Grab

You get *Black File 04* FREE with this book (see the
Table of Contents for details).

Midnight Burn

Angel of Darkness Book 04

Steve N. Lee

Copyright

Copyright © Steve N. Lee 2015

www.SteveNLeeBooks.com

The characters and events in this book are fictitious and any resemblance to real people, living or dead, is purely coincidental.

All rights reserved. No part of this work may be reproduced, stored in a retrieval system, or transmitted in any form or by any means — electronic, mechanical, photocopying, recording or otherwise — without the prior permission of the publisher.

Published by Blue Zoo, Yorkshire, England.

Midnight Burn

Chapter 01

IN THE SHADOWS of her apartment building's doorway, a dark figure lurked.

"Oh, hell." That was all she needed. Slouched in the back of the yellow cab, Amelia buried her face in her hands and heaved a great breath. She didn't need to see the figure clearly – she knew who it was. And she knew if he hit her once more – just once – she was out of here. And this time, she meant it.

Raking her fingers back through her long brown hair, she groaned. Arriving home nearly two hours later than she'd agreed, she'd hoped to be able to creep in unnoticed while Ethan was asleep. Not because she didn't want to disturb him, but because she didn't want a fight. Well, that idea was shot.

As the cab swung in to park behind Ethan's rusting pickup truck, she dabbed her crotch with a crumbled tissue to remove any lingering traces of the guy from the bar, and with it, any lingering traces of the escape plan he provided. She smiled. Those ten minutes in the toilet stall were the highlight of her week. She couldn't remember the last time she'd felt so good. Felt so wanted. Felt worth something.

She noticed the dark eyes of the taxi driver staring through his rearview mirror. She knew he didn't have an angle to see her hand inside her panties, but he could see enough. The last thing she needed was him thinking she was coming on to him. Ewww. That beard scraping her face raw? And that gigantic belly pounding into her? Oh, God, she'd puke.

She arched an eyebrow at him. "A little privacy, huh?"

The driver looked away.

Seconds later, the cab stopped and the driver turned to her. "Fourteen fifty."

His accent was thick. Foreign. She didn't know where he was from and she didn't care.

As she yanked the door open, she pushed two scrunched bills at him. "I got ten bucks."

His dark-skinned hand caught her bony wrist. He was so big compared to her, it was like an adult holding a child by the arm.

He glowered. "Fourteen fifty!"

She snatched her hand away. "Hey, you got a free floor show."

She clambered out and into the shadows of her building, its six-story patchwork of darkened windows, broken only occasionally by a lit one, suggesting that the city that never sleeps actually did.

The taxi driver clambered out too. "Another four dollars fifty."

A cool wind biting at the summer's night, the chilly air coaxed goose bumps from her bare thighs. Her yellow skirt might look fabulous but it offered as much warmth as a silk scarf tied around her waist. She hugged herself, bouncing gently from side to side.

She said, "Look, that's all I got."

"Then maybe I call the police."

"Call. You think they'll give a crap?" She turned to leave.

From out of the shadows, a guy with muscles oozing out of his white undershirt marched towards her.

Under her breath, she said, "Oh, shit."

Ethan scowled at her. "You know what time it is?"

Meanwhile, the taxi driver had appeared beside her. "Another four fifty. Or there'll be trouble."

Ethan turned to him, arms folded over a proud chest. His stare drilled into the driver for a moment before he said anything. "Trouble? Over five bucks? Is it worth five bucks to get your face all messed up?"

The driver backed away, hands up, shoulders hunched. "Okay, okay. No police. No trouble."

"Damn right." Ethan's scowl swung back to Amelia. "Well?"

"Well what?"

With his cab between them, the driver obviously felt more courageous. He pointed at each of them. "You I won't forget."

"Is that so?" Ethan stabbed a finger at the driver, his bicep bulging. "You want a keepsake, just in case?"

He slammed a kick into the taxi's rear door, denting it.

The driver shouted, "The police, they give a crap now!"

Ethan lunged, as if he were about to race around the car at the driver.

Frantic, the driver fumbled opening his door, then jumped in his cab and shot away.

Ethan turned back to her. "So this is what I get for letting you go out with your friends?"

"*Letting me?* You *let* me go out?" She snickered.

"Think this is funny, huh?" He had that wild glare in his eyes – the one that always led to bruises appearing on her body which she had to lie to her friends about.

She flinched. "No, no. I'm sorry. Honest." She shrank back from him. Tried to be even smaller than she already was.

An old man with a cane limped towards them – the neighborhood weirdo all the local kids called Hop-along.

Though she always slapped on cosmetics to hide the evidence, the whole block knew Ethan was violent. Being in charge of the Neighborhood Watch, surely Hop-along would see how menacing Ethan was being and help her.

She caught Hop-along's eye. Silently pleaded for help.

The old guy immediately looked away. Stepped off the curb to cross the road. Never said a word.

She was on her own. As usual.

Further down the street, red brake lights caught her eye as her taxi slowed and hung a left. She ached to be sitting in it.

Ethan grabbed her by the arm. Shook her. "Hey, I'm talking here. Pull that silent shit and don't blame me for what happens."

She looked up into his eyes. "Ethan, really, I'm sorry. I just lost track of time. Okay?"

"Lose track of your cell phone as well?"

"I turned it off. I was having a good time."

"Oh, yeah? Who with?"

She wriggled free of his grip. "You know who. I told you. The girls – Becks and Trish and the others."

"And…?"

"And what? That's it."

Ethan glowered at her, arms folded, his biceps gleaming under the streetlights. "So, no one else?"

"No. Just them. So can we go in now? It's goddamn freezing." She reached out to touch Ethan's arm, but he shrugged her off.

He said, "So how come Blaine saw you with a guy in Shades?"

Oh, hell. "Blaine? Blaine! You believe a screwed-up dopehead like Blaine over me? Jesus, most days that guy wouldn't recognize his own mother if he was banging her."

"So what's this?" Ethan thrust his phone at her. It displayed a photo of her cozily chatting with a man at a bar, her hand on his arm. It was dark and her face was mostly obscured, but it was clearly her.

11

"That's not me." She pushed the phone away.

"No? Same hair. Same skirt."

"Like I'm the only girl with brown hair and a yellow skirt? Jesus, Ethan, get a grip."

His eyes widening into that glare again, she knew she'd pushed him too far.

She smiled. "Look, let me fetch some beers and smokes from the store" – she stroked her hand along his forearm and gazed into his eyes – "we'll put on some music and I'll show you how much I missed you tonight."

He pulled back again. "Don't go trying that sweet talk shit. This time I got proof."

"So what do you want, Ethan? To smack me around a bit? Then say you're sorry so I'll blow you?"

He leaned right down in her face. "Don't push it. I'm warning you."

"Warn who you like." She turned away, praying he wouldn't lash out at her. "I'm buying beer. Drink it or don't drink it. See if I care."

She flounced down the street, hoping a trip to the store would give her time to concoct a decent story. She'd call Becks for backup too.

He shouted after her. "Don't think this is over, because it ain't!"

Christ, was she sick of men walking all over her. Well, that was going to change. She deserved better so she was going to have better and to hell with anyone who got in her way.

She marched toward the end of the block. Now, how was she going to twist her story so Ethan would buy it long enough for her to figure out what to do next?

At the corner, she turned left onto Chiltern. The wind gusted through the concrete canyon. She shivered and tightly hugged her arms around her chest.

Ducking into the setback doorway of A Taste of Napoli, she hunched over her cupped hands to light a cigarette. The wind extinguished her lighter. She tried again. But failed again. "Goddamn it."

She thought she heard a voice, so she glanced towards the street, but she saw no one.

She tried her cigarette for a third time.

Something touched her right upper arm. She jumped. Pulled away. As far into the corner of the darkened doorway as she could.

Chapter 02

SILHOUETTED BY A streetlight stood a tiny, lopsided figure. "Is everything alright?"

"I've got a knife!" Amelia hadn't, but the figure didn't know that.

The figure moved nearer, a hand out toward her. "It's okay. It's me: Mr. Ridley. I just wanted to check you're okay."

It was Hop-along, the old man with the limp who could've helped her but didn't.

Batting his hand away, she said, "What's your fucking game? Keep your hands to yourself, you old pervert." She bustled passed him back onto the street.

"Jesus, you're old enough to be my grandpa." She scowled at him. Men, what the hell was wrong with them?

He said, "I'm sorry. I was only—"

"Only trying to cop a feel. Hell, I'm not surprised all the kids think you're a creep. Do you try to feel them up, too, you fucking pedophile?"

His wizened face hung in shock. He looked as pathetic as a dog that had taken a dump on the carpet and knew it was in for it.

He hobbled closer. "Please, Amelia, that's a horrible thing to say. I'm only trying to help."

"Trying to take advantage, more like." She snatched her phone from her purse and pointed it at him. "Well, not of me, you're not. I'm gonna put your photo online. Tell everyone what a pervert you are. See you chased out of the neighborhood. Have Child Services at your door. Fucking pedophile!"

"Please, Amelia. Don't." Cowering, he crossed his arms in front of his face to hide from the camera in her phone. "I'm sorry. I didn't mean to upset you." He backed away.

He looked like he was about to cry. Christ, talk about sad. A grown man crying over names he'd been called. But it served him right. He should've helped her. Neighborhood Watch her ass.

It was usually men making her feel weak and useless – it was good to finally know what it was like to be on the other side. Watching him squirm, she felt strong, dominant, unstoppable.

As she walked backwards, she kept her phone aimed at him. She chanted, "Pedophile. Pedophile. Pedophile."

He stood gawking at her. Frozen with shock.

"See you on Facebook, pedo." Continuing down the sidewalk, she laughed. The night no longer felt so chill. Her luck no longer felt so bad. She strolled toward the store, head high.

As she neared it, she realized the car parked across the street from Patel's Convenience Store was a taxi cab. She thought nothing of it, until she was almost even with it and spotted a large dent in the rear door – a dent that looked as if someone had kicked the metal panel.

The interior was too dark to see if anyone was inside, but she wasn't going to let that sleazy driver have the satisfaction of hassling her again when he saw she was lying about having no money.

Crossing the road behind the cab, and empowered by abusing the old man, she paused in the middle of the street just long enough to flip the darkened cab the finger. Laughing, she headed into the store.

Back on the street moments later, she bounced down the sidewalk for home, with four cans of beer in a white plastic bag.

The darkened taxi was still parked, but there was no sign of the old man. She'd felt powerful after her fight with Hop-along, but now, her adrenaline drained, the street felt so much darker, so much more threatening.

She glanced back at the taxi shrouded in gloom. The driver was a big guy, a giant compared to her. Still, with his blubbery belly she'd easily outrun him if he tried anything.

She crossed the street and rounded the corner. No matter what trouble you were in, once you were within spitting distance of your home, you knew everything was going to be just fine. Usually. Walking along the deserted street, Amelia shivered again. But not from the cold. This time, she shivered because she was sure she wasn't alone.

She spun around.

Scoured the shadows.

Gloom hung in doorways. Blackness bled out of alleys.

She scanned the darkness.

Nothing moved.

In a city of eight million people, the silence was unearthly.

Amelia backed away, peering into the shadows. She couldn't help but feel someone was watching. Someone was waiting. But who? And waiting for what?

The street she knew so well suddenly felt so much darker, so much lonelier.

Turning for home, she quickened her pace.

It was just her imagination. There was nothing there. What was she? A goddamn child?

But she shuddered. And again glanced over her shoulder.

There was someone there. Somewhere. She goddamn knew it.

Again, she quickened her pace.

Marching toward her building, she looked at the windows of Hop-along's apartment. Because of her fight with Ethan, Hop-along had born the savage brunt of her frustration. He hadn't deserved that. He was weird, yes, but he meant well. And like he could've helped. An old cripple taking on Ethan? Hell, Ethan would've busted up his other leg just for the hell of it. No, it wasn't Hop-along's fault. And calling him a pedophile was a horrible thing to have done. She'd apologize to him the next time she saw him.

A shudder ran down her spine. She looked behind her again. It was weird how people could tell when someone was watching them. Weird. And scary. She squinted, straining to pick out any figure hiding in the blackness.

Still nothing. Nothing but looming shadows.

Hell, she wished the little old man would pop up now with a cheery word and that crooked smile of his. She was sure someone was stalking her. Lurking in the darkness, just out of sight.

If she hadn't fought with Ethan, she'd call him and make him come down to meet her, even though she could now see her apartment building. It wouldn't be the first time he'd busted up some whack-job for hassling her.

"Oh, hell." *Ethan.* What was she going to tell him? In fact, would she be able to tell him anything if he'd flown into one of his rages because she'd dared to walk away while he was still talking?

Her pace slowed to a crawl. She needed a good story. A convincing story. She couldn't go rushing home until she had one he couldn't rip apart.

Okay, she'd tell him the guy in the bar was an old work colleague. No – a gay work colleague. Oh, yeah, that was it. Say she'd shown him Ethan's photo and he'd said what great muscles Ethan had.

Oh, damn it. Ethan wasn't the smartest guy she'd ever dated, but he wasn't that dumb. What the hell was she going to tell him?

Dawdling to stall for time, her door just yards away, she again took out her phone. Becks would know what to do – she had a sixth sense when it came to lying to guys. But Amelia didn't just need advice, she needed to hear a friendly voice – whoever was following her was creeping her out.

Amelia flicked through her address book and hit Becks's number.

The phone to her ear, Amelia thought she heard a noise behind her.

The hair on the back of her neck prickled.

She whipped around and—

Chapter 03

SITTING ON THE ground beneath her favorite willow tree, Tess slowly exhaled.

Amid a gentle mist clinging to the water's tranquil surface, ducks quacked on the small lake. The sun hovered above the tree line but the world was yet sleepy, chilled, still.

At the foot of her tree, Tess sat deep in meditation – completely enveloped in a world of her own making. But then, didn't everyone live in their own tiny world? While global affairs were beyond an individual's grasp, the everyday world a person created for themselves was under their complete control: their choices shaped their life. Unfortunately, like every other person on the planet, Tess often made the wrong choices, so her world was far from the utopia her philosophy decreed it had the potential to be.

Her breathing steady, eyes closed, Tess slowly emerged from her meditation. A sound had disturbed her. A sound unbefitting her favorite place. A sound of distress. Something was wrong.

With blue eyes as sparkling as the dew-laden grass, she scanned the park for the cause of the problem. Nothing.

Unfurling from her lotus position, she drew a deep breath and then stood. For a few seconds, she shook her muscles loose and worked her joints.

Snagging her black backpack from the grass, she turned toward the small bay in which rowboats could be rented during the park's official opening hours. She glided along the dry dirt trail with the grace of a dancer who'd graduated top of her year at Juilliard.

Again, a noise shattered the stillness – an eruption of honking. But it wasn't the usual traffic in the background. No, this was something living.

Rounding a clump of conifers, Tess saw three men on a narrow wooden jetty which crawled out over the lake on hefty moss-covered posts. The jetty's worn timbers creaked and groaned under the men's antics. From their dress, and their being in their late teens, early twenties, she guessed they had been partying all night and, on their way home, had invented a game for some last-minute fun. Unfortunately, the game seemed extremely one-sided.

Another pebble hit the lake's limpid waters. It skipped once, twice, three times and then...

Honking erupted once more.

Ducks near the far shore honked and squawked and quacked as the missile skimmed the surface between them and then plopped into the depths.

The three guys whooped with disappointment tempered with delight.

With a brown pug in a red dog coat ambling alongside her, an old lady approached the men. Tess couldn't hear what she said to them, but she didn't need to. The men turned towards the lady, grimacing.

The nearer one, a tall, gangly guy with a leather jacket, gave her the finger. "What's it to do with you, you nosey old cow? Fuck off!"

At the end of the jetty, a short, fat guy skimmed another stone across the water. Frantic quacks suggested something had been hit.

The fat guy shouted, "Score!"

All three guys cheered and laughed.

The old lady must have said something else, because the gangly guy pulled his arm back and aimed a stone at her dog. "You gonna fuck off? Or do I have to make you?"

The lady scurried back along the path, almost dragging her poor little dog off its feet in her hurry to get away.

Tess huffed. She had to be somewhere. Urgently. The only reason she'd stopped off here was to mentally prepare herself for the ordeal to come. She should really walk away from this. But could she?

One sunny afternoon years ago, Tess had lounged in the shade of a cherry tree playing Xiangqi on a wobbly oak table with Cheng Chao-an. With sunlight dappling the Chinese chessboard and a cool breeze gliding up the valley to the ridge on which they were sitting, she'd felt peace. True peace. The kind of peace people dreamed about after seeing it in a feel-good movie but never truly believed existed outside Hollywood fantasy.

But there was a problem with peace – it never lasted.

Cheng moved one of his canons and captured her last elephant.

Staring at the pieces scattered across the board, Tess realized she was just two or three moves away from losing yet another game to the master of Wudangshan Temple.

Her shoulders slumped and before she knew it, she blurted out, "Oh, I hate this stupid goddamn game."

Cheng didn't understand English, but he obviously recognized her anguish from her tone and body language. As he moved one of his chariots across the river to threaten her general, she was sure the tiniest of smiles flickered across his craggy face. Not that he enjoyed winning. Teaching, however, was a different story.

In Mandarin, he said, "We each create our own versions of heaven and hell through the choices we make."

Almost everything Cheng said had many layers, a point she'd quickly picked up during the two months she'd been studying philosophy under him. This remark was no exception. If she'd won the game, she'd have congratulated herself for being a skilled player and making all the right moves. However, having lost, similarly, she had only herself to 'congratulate' for making all the wrong moves. Likewise in life, a person chose all the moves they made so they alone were responsible for the resulting predicaments in which they found themselves.

Tess neared the jetty which stretched out over the park's lake. Today, would her students appreciate the beauty in the teaching she was about to share?

Breathing hard, the old lady patted her pale face with a cotton handkerchief, all the color having drained from her complexion.

An ordinary person looking on would have recognized this loss of color as fear, even cowardice. Something to disdain. But that person would be wrong. Under stressful situations, the brain released adrenaline to aid with any necessary fight or flight, one side effect of which was the blood draining from the extremities to boost the supply to vital organs, which meant the skin looking pale. It was simple biology.

And that was why most people fell apart in stressful situations – they didn't understand their own bodies, their own reactions, so they couldn't grasp what was happening to them. The result was they either froze or panicked because they'd let their rational mind be replaced by a basic survival instinct. And an inability to make a reasoned decision seldom led to a favorable outcome.

Again, it was all down to choice. How the world crumbled without it.

Now Tess had a choice of her own to make: to walk away from men abusing people and animals unable to defend themselves, or…

Watching the three men tormenting the ducks, Tess felt her heart start to race. She knew if she let it, her adrenaline would spike, her heartbeat would skyrocket, she'd lose motor skills and rational thought, and... her world would come crashing down.

Tess drew in a deep breath for four seconds, held it for another four, and then blew it out over four seconds. Slowing her breathing would slow her body's reaction, slow the release of adrenaline, slow the onset of panic. It was a simple technique with which to face hazardous situations. A simple technique that could see you walk away with a spring in your step instead of being carried away with a sheet over your face.

Tess stopped in front of the old lady. "You okay?"

"Oh Lord, I can't hold my hand steady. Look." She held a trembling hand up.

"Do you have a cell phone?"

"Yes, but I come here every day. If I call the police, heaven knows what they'll do to me and Charlie." She looked down at her pug, which looked as upset as she did, though that being the breed's normal expression, it was somewhat misleading.

"Don't call the police. Call an ambulance."

"Thank you, but I don't need an ambulance. I just need to go home and sit down."

"Trust me. Call an ambulance." Tess walked by her toward the jetty. And the three delinquents.

"Don't go down there," the old lady called after her. "It's not worth it."

Chapter 04

AS TESS STROLLED toward the jetty, her heart pounding, her mind a whirl of scenarios each ending with her in a pool of blood on the ground, she used her four-second breathing technique to steady her heartbeat and her mind. Clarity. She needed clarity if she was to survive a dangerous situation without injury.

Out in the lake, a lump of bloody feathers silently bobbed on the water. Walk away? As if that were a choice open to her.

Today, it was ducks. Tomorrow, it could be dogs. Next week, it could be kids. Not worth it? Man, was it worth it.

From the grassy lakeshore, she picked up two stones. Without looking, she rolled them around in her hand to know their shape and weight.

On the jetty, the gangly guy pulled his arm back to skim another pebble at the ducks.

A stone cracked into the side of his head.

"Ahhh, fuck!" He hunched over, his hand naturally cupping his wound. When he took it away and looked at it, he swore again. He turned, scowling.

Tess stood at the start of the jetty, just looking at him. She tossed her other stone a few inches into the air and then caught it.

He shouted, "You fucking mental bitch!"

"You know" – she gestured to the birds on the water – "the ducks were right – this is fun." She smiled.

He stalked towards her. "You'll pay for that, you crazy bitch."

"Hey, don't be like that. They really want to play with you guys. The thing is they think the teams are unfair, so they've asked me to play on their side. That okay?" She threw the second stone at the gangly guy.

He twisted away. Too late. The stone hit him square in the back.

He growled like an angry animal.

Spun.

Stormed toward her.

His face twisted with rage, he said, "I'm gonna break your fucking legs, bitch."

She waited. Unmoving. He must have thought it was his birthday it was going to be so easy.

The auburn-haired fat guy at the end of the jetty shouted, "Do her, Gazza. Fucking do the bitch."

Gazza grabbed her jacket's lapel with his left hand and heaved his right fist far back to his shoulder. It was obvious what he was intending to do – smash her face to a bloody pulp with a heavy right cross.

This was when an ordinary person would be scared. This was when an ordinary person would run like hell. This was when an ordinary person would soil themselves.

She threw her hands up. "Whoa, whoa, whoa, whoa..."

He hesitated.

She said, "You really wanna do this?"

Tess didn't need to hear his answer. She felt his grip on her jacket tighten. Saw his right fist pull back a couple more inches. Sensed his body tense for action.

Yes, choices. It was all about choices.

He growled. Unleashed a crashing punch toward Tess's head.

She snapped her right arm up, bent, elbow jutting straight out in front of her face.

Gazza's hand smashed into the point of her elbow, one of the hardest parts of the human body.

He yelped like a dog that had been stomped on.

He pulled back. Cradled his hurt hand in his other.

Tess slammed a kick into his gut.

With a great wheeze, he doubled up. Staggered back.

With barely an effort, she shoved his shoulder.

He toppled into the lake.

The jetty was only five feet wide, so she knew they could only come at her one at a time. She slunk forward.

In a red shirt, the skinny guy who'd been in the middle of the three shuffled toward her. Fists at chest height. Knees bent. Body angled diagonally with his left leg forward. It was a trained fighter's stance.

When just a pace away from her, the guy shifted his weight onto his front leg and twisted that foot inwards.

He might as well have held up a placard declaring his intentions.

The guy spun backwards.

Shot a kick straight up at her head.

And a damn fine kick it was. It would've looked great in a movie. But for a real-life street fight?

Tess's head was no longer where he'd aimed. Already dropped to one knee, she slammed the heel of her right palm into the most exposed part of his body – his groin.

He gasped, eyes wide.

As the guy crumpled, Tess bounced up. Her elbow slammed up into his jaw. Bone crunched.

Arms splayed, the skinny guy crashed backwards into the water.

Tess swung her gaze over to the fat guy at the end of the jetty.

Mouth agape, the fat guy stared at her. His face was so pale, his auburn hair looked all but fluorescent in comparison.

She stalked toward him.

Face twisted with panic, he backed up. Inched closer to the end of the jetty. Teetered on the edge.

Tess crept forward. Watched his hands. His feet. Where his gaze fell.

Even the most inept of fighters could land a lucky punch if their opponent was inattentive. There was no room for arrogance or complacency on the street.

Probably looking for escape, the fat guy spun to his right – water. To his left – water. Behind him – water. On three sides there was nothing but water. On the fourth, nothing but pain.

Tess feigned punching him.

He dodged.

She feigned another shot.

Again, he needlessly dodged.

Obviously exasperated, he lunged. He didn't so much punch as merely flail an arm in her general direction.

She sidestepped. Twisting her hip to get her full weight behind it, she slammed her open hand into the side of his head.

He staggered right.

Regaining his balance, he flailed his other arm at her.

Again, she dodged. A mighty slap cracked into the other side of his head.

He staggered left. Teetering on the jetty's edge, he caught himself just before he fell into the water.

He held his head and then shook it as if to clear it.

Gulping great breaths, he glanced at her, at his two drenched friends, and then back to her.

Tess drilled her stare into him. "The way I see it, you've got two choices." She clenched her fists, raising them into a guard position similar to that of a boxer.

Again he spun for escape – to his right, left, behind him.

He turned back to her.

"Fuck this." He spun.

Leapt from the end of the jetty.

Crashed into the lake.

Tess said, "Smart choice."

She looked at the three guys in the water. They stared up at her, pale faced, whimpering, clutching their injuries.

She nodded. "Good game, guys. Shall we say same time next week? I'm always here."

She sauntered along the jetty and back onto the asphalt path. She'd have liked to have thought the three guys would reflect on this encounter and, through deep empathy, develop a greater appreciation for life – all life. But she didn't live in la-la-lu-lu land. Still, at least, they'd think twice before abusing anyone or anything else for fear of who may be lurking in the shadows, watching.

Goggle-eyed, the old lady stared as Tess approached. The woman's mouth gaped so wide, Tess could all but see the filled cavities in her lower teeth.

But the woman didn't smile. Didn't thank Tess. Didn't congratulate her for seeing justice done. Holding her white handkerchief to her face, the woman's hand trembled even more than when Tess had first met her.

The path was wide enough for five people to walk comfortably side by side, but the old lady stepped off it and onto the grass to let Tess pass. It was as if she'd seen a vicious beast. A monster run amok.

Around the world, most women were caregivers, nurturers, child bearers, victims, healers, homemakers, followers, mediators… Women were many things, but the one thing they were not was predators.

Psychologically, sociologically, and physiologically women had evolved to be the gentler sex. Both voluntarily and because it had been demanded of them. They turned mere places to live into homes; they dedicated their lives to the good of their social group; they sacrificed their goals for the sake of others.

Most women did not seek vengeance.

They did not reap justice.

They did not kill.

So was it Tess who was the monster?

She glanced back. The old lady hadn't moved. Except to turn and watch Tess leaving. Tess would've liked to think the lady was simply curious, but it was far more than that. The old lady had been more afraid of her than of those three delinquents.

So was she a monster?

Today, Tess hadn't killed anyone. Hadn't even maimed anyone. Those guys would suffer for a few weeks, but make a full recovery. All she had done was be present to witness the choices each of them had made.

If they had chosen a different path – chosen to be home in bed instead of terrorizing animals in a park – there would have been no violence. The violence had only occurred because of the path each of them had chosen to walk. Even up to that last few seconds before the violence erupted, they'd had the opportunity to make a different choice. They had chosen not to. Every path reached an end. The violent encounter with Tess had been at the end of theirs.

Tess shook her head. No, she wasn't a monster. She'd done the right thing. And she'd do it again. And keep on doing it until there was no longer the need. But when would that be?

Everywhere she went she found injustice. Found the greedy exploiting the vulnerable. Found scum abusing the innocent.

It was endless. What would she find next?

Who would she find deserving of the justice only she could bring?

Chapter 05

WITH YELLOW CRIME scene tape closing off the alleyway between two apartment buildings, the police might as well have sent out invitations to every busybody within a five-block radius. Not that there was anything to see; the crime, whatever it was, was hidden around the corner, where protruding scaffolding suggested some form of renovation was underway.

From the front of the crowd of people, Tess stared at the graffiti on the side of the right-hand building. In blue, black and red letters five feet tall, the main element spelled out ISAAC.Z. The second *A* completely blacked out one of the building's windows. Either someone didn't live there or was too afraid of Isaac Z to scrub his tag away.

She looked at the young male officer guarding the perimeter. "Excuse me?"

Nothing.

She waited a moment, then tried again. "Excuse me?"

With a slight squint, the cop looked at her and then meandered over. "Can I help you, ma'am?"

Ma'am!? Since when did she stop being a miss? Was that what happened as you approached thirty? The worst part was he looked no younger than she felt she did.

She smiled. "Who's the detective in charge, please?"

"That would be Detective McEleroy, ma'am."

"Pete McEleroy?"

"Yes, ma'am."

"Could I speak with him, please?"

"As you'll appreciate, he's kind of busy right now."

"Can you tell him Tess Williams is here?"

"Do you have information about the crime, Ms. Williams?"

"If you just tell him I'm here, please."

The officer studied her eyes for a second.

"Just a moment." He turned and said something into his radio that she couldn't hear. A moment later, at the other end of the alley, a portly man waddled out from behind the building and waved for her to join him. The young officer lifted the tape to shoulder height. "There you go, ma'am."

"Thank you." She ducked under and marched up the alleyway. The portly detective waddled a few steps toward her. A noticeable smile crept across his face. He tried to hide it by rubbing a hand over his face and then back through his graying hair.

On reaching him, she smiled and shook his outstretched hand. "I see the cheeseburger diet is working its magic, Mac."

He laughed and proudly rubbed his gut. "Gained six pounds so far this year." He turned for the back of the building again. "So how are things with you?"

"Oh, you know. We'll have to have a drink sometime soon and catch up."

"That would be, er, nice."

She saw him try to stifle a smirk again. No surprise, really – it wasn't every day an overweight fifty-five-year-old cop got to secretly lay a woman half his age with the toned physique of an Olympic swimmer.

"'Nice', huh?" She raised an eyebrow.

He glanced around for who might be listening. "Yeah, you know…"

She smiled to let him know she was messing with him. She didn't want his colleagues learning of their relationship as it would cramp her style, and he couldn't risk it – if his wife learned of it, she'd take his kids, his house, and most of his paycheck.

But she liked that he'd squirmed. It meant she still had access to what she needed: information. And access was all that mattered if she was going to do her job.

Approaching the corner of the alley, she said, "So what have we got here?"

"Put it this way, you ain't gonna be rushing to eat anytime soon."

She turned the corner. And there was the victim. Unusually for Tess, she gasped and stopped dead.

As if reading from a somewhat bland menu, Mac said, "Amelia Ortega, twenty-one, local resident. Found by some kids playing hide and seek. We have no time of death and we're still trying to establish cause. From the blunt force injuries, it looks like she was beaten with something – maybe a rock hammer or some similar tool – so death could be from that or…" He gestured to the body. "This is one real sicko."

At a glacial pace, one forensics officer hovered around the body, taking photos from a variety of angles, while a colleague crouched examining some kind of marking on the asphalt which Tess couldn't make out. A bald man hunched over the body, scrutinizing the face and throat.

Tess winced as she looked at Amelia. Lying face up, Amelia 'hung' in midair. Impaled through the crotch on a horizontal scaffolding pole, her arms and legs dangled down to either side behind her. To support her, the pole obviously extended deep into her body cavity, so must have caused massive internal damage. Not only that, but from where her mouth and lower jaw should have been burst forth bloody pulp and jagged white bone, as if someone had tried to impale her the other way around to start with but only succeeded in mashing up her face.

"Jesus." Tess stared at the body dangling in the air like a dead bird a child had picked up with a stick. This was not just a straightforward murder. This was something else entirely. But what?

"How deep does the pole go?"

Mac shrugged. "We don't know yet. But it must be quite a way. I tell you, whoever did this was either real strong or real pissed."

In times of extreme stress, natural strength wasn't necessary: rage could turn an ordinary person into an absolute Goliath. She knew that from her own experience. And, luckily, she knew how to harness such power.

With the majority of homicides being committed by a person the victim knows, there were the usual suspects to consider. Tess said, "There a guy in the picture?"

"And that's where it gets interesting – live-in boyfriend Ethan Michael Dumfries has conveniently gone AWOL."

"Priors?"

"Two years ago, his girlfriend at that time made a complaint for assault, but then refused to follow through, so it was dropped."

There was someone else at the scene, though. Someone Tess didn't recognize. Someone taking notes while crouched beside the bald ME. She knew who should've been there, and though she couldn't get a good look at this guy because he had his back to her, it was definitely not who she was expecting to see with Mac.

She tossed a glance toward the stranger. "Old Horowitz finally get his year-round fishing vacation?"

"Sadly." Mac nodded. "This guy's a transfer from uptown. He's doing okay."

But a newcomer wasn't the important issue here. Tess looked at the victim.

From what was left of Amelia's face, and from her slender limbs and Hollywood-flat stomach, Tess could tell Amelia would've been very popular. Maybe too popular. There was an obvious question, so Tess asked it.

"Was she raped?"

"Hard to say." He shrugged. "That could be one reason for doing that to a body – trying to hide the evidence. The lab results should clear that up."

From beside the ME, the transfer-from-uptown guy meandered toward them, his gait slow but solid, upright, purposeful. With a full head of thick black hair and a muscular build, he looked like Mac must once have looked before the ceaseless cases and endless junk food took their toll.

Tess cringed. Oh, God, she knew this interloper, alright – the pompous dick from the Pool Cleaner job who had all but advised her to take up flower arranging on the grounds that she was a helpless woman.

On catching Tess's eye, the transfer-from-uptown guy looked equally thrown, though she guessed it was for a different reason. He scanned Tess, obviously wondering why she, a mere member of the public, deserved access to their inner sanctum.

Chapter 06

FOR A MOMENT, Tess and the new guy stood facing each other like rival gunslingers in a Wild West saloon, each warily sizing-up the other. Luckily, the local sheriff was on hand to ensure the encounter remained peaceful.

Mac gestured to each of them in turn. "Tess Williams, meet Detective Josh Hardy. A transfer from uptown."

Not wanting to let her body language give away her displeasure, she resumed her jovial demeanor as quickly as she could.

Smiling, Tess held out her hand. "Hello again."

Josh shook it. "Miss Williams."

"You two know each other? Have you worked together?" asked Mac.

"No, no," said Tess. "It was just in passing." She could kick herself. Would it have hurt her to phone Josh after he'd been kind enough to offer to coach her in self-defense all those months back? She'd known he might be useful at a later date, so why the hell couldn't she just have gritted her teeth and let him play the hero by giving her some free pointers. Hell, she'd scalded her mouth on the coffee he'd bought her she'd been so eager to get away.

Josh frowned at her. "So what? You're a cop? You never said anything."

"No, I, er…" Tess fumbled for the right words.

Mac said, "Tess has proven invaluable in the past. She has a knack for digging up information we can only dream of finding."

Obviously suspicious, Josh scrutinized Tess. His slate-blue eyes stared intently. Cold, yet strangely drawing. He said, "Some kind of consultant?"

Mac shock his head. "It's complicated. Don't bother about it. Just feel free to speak openly in front of her."

Josh still studied Tess. "If you say so."

"I do," said Mac.

Tess gestured to the dead body. "So, any signs of foul play?"

Josh's jaw dropped. "Excuse me?" He pointed back at the suspended body. "You don't think—"

A huge belly laugh burst from Mac.

Josh looked at him, then back at Tess. She stood, unflinchingly serious.

"Ohhh." Josh nodded, smiling. "Okay. Yeah, I'm the new guy. You got me. I can see now why you keep getting your ass kicked."

Tess winked at Josh. Making a good impression now could serve her well in the future if he was Mac's

41

new partner, and humor was a great icebreaker. A quick wit could quickly and easily endear you to a complete stranger. Or to someone you'd inadvertently offended.

"Am I missing something?" Mac looked from one of them to the other for an explanation.

Tess smiled. "No, Detective Hardy bumped into me one day after a bad sparring session at my self-defense class, is all."

"Oh, okay." Mac beckoned for Josh to reveal what he'd noted. "So, what we got?"

Josh glanced at his notes. "From the temperature of the body, the M.E. estimates the time of death to be between one and three thirty this morning, though he's hopeful he can narrow that down later. The blood pattern suggests the victim was killed someplace else, possibly with a single blow to the throat, and then dragged here."

"Any insight on why the elaborate display?" Mac asked.

Josh shrugged. "Maybe it's gang related."

Tess shook her head. "Unless she's some gangbanger's girl and been caught banging someone from a rival gang, this isn't gang related. It's way too personal. To be so brutal, the killer was either punishing her and sending a message to someone else, or he's insane and believes he's an artist with this his masterpiece."

Sweeping his hand from Josh toward Tess, Mac said, "What did I tell you?"

She knew Mac would've had that same thought, but she appreciated the vote of confidence he'd just shown to quell any concerns the younger detective might have harbored about her.

Tess scribbled all the other available details in her notebook and then dropped it into her backpack. To say her goodbyes, she touched Mac's forearm. She noticed Josh's gaze flick down to follow what she'd done. Good: keeping Mac on edge would ensure he stayed nicely compliant and amenable.

"I'll check back with you later," said Tess. "Maybe arrange that drink."

Ambling back down the alley toward the street, Tess thought about the old lady in the park who'd been so horrified by Tess's aptitude for violence that she'd looked at her as if she were a monster. Tess could understand such a viewpoint – it was too unusual for a woman to be able to do what she did. More crucially, it was too unusual for a woman to use such brutality with such calmness. That was the crux of the problem – Tess's calmness. The calmness of a psychopath. Someone who had no empathy for others and so saw no problem in inflicting unbelievable suffering upon them. A monster.

In the old lady's world, there were ordinary people and then there were monsters, with no gray area blurring the distinction between the two. A serial killer was a monster. A rapist? A monster. A pedophile? A monster. A monster was simply a monster. No gray area. No questions. No doubts, only fact. That logic meant the old lady saw Tess not as an ordinary, decent person like herself, but someone more akin to the monster who'd killed Amelia.

Those three guys in the park, on the other hand, weren't monsters. They were just ordinary guys, like hundreds of guys in hundreds of cities. Cruel, yes. Irresponsible, yes. Unthinking, yes. But explainable, understandable, even relatable.

Tess?

How could people relate to her, to what she was, to what she did?

To the old lady, indeed, to the majority of the population, a woman who could inflict such carnage, without even flinching, could be nothing but a monster.

Tess sighed. Was she a monster? Could so many people really be so wrong? Would the world be a better place without her?

Tess pictured Amelia impaled on the metal pole.

A better place without her?

The only time the world would be a better place was when it no longer had a need for her and what she could do.

That time was not now.

On the contrary, now, it was time for her to do what she did best – be what some might call a monster.

Chapter 07

AT THE BOTTOM of the alley, the police officer lifted the yellow crime scene tape and Tess ducked under it again.

She fished her cell phone from her backpack and slipped it out of its little pouch. Made of RF shielding materials, the pouch meant no one could trace her through her phone like they did in the movies. It irritated her how often some James Bond-wannabe saved the world from total obliteration by managing to trace the bad guy through his phone. Hell, all the villain had to do was blow a whopping seventy bucks on one of these little pouches and he could stand on top of the most powerful cell tower in Manhattan and even the NSA's biggest supercomputer wouldn't spot him. Talk about handing it to the hero on a plate.

She scanned the numbers in her phone. Where to start?

She half-heard someone say something but was too engrossed in her phone to pay any heed.

A gentle voice disturbed her. "I said, 'excuse me,' dear."

She glanced up. "Hmm?"

A little old man stood before her. "Do you happen to know what's going on, please?" He gestured to the alleyway.

"Oh, er, sorry. Miles away. Yes, it's a crime scene. There's been a homicide." She went back to her phone.

"It's not someone from around here, is it?"

"I'm sorry, but I'm not at liberty to say."

"I run the local neighborhood watch, so maybe I can help."

She looked up. Maybe he could help. She smiled, putting her phone in its pouch and into the inside pocket of her black leather jacket. "I'm sorry. You were saying?"

He said, "Are you with the police?"

"No, but I'm looking into this case."

"A reporter?"

"Not exactly. Now, about your neighborhood watch."

"I actually started it nearly thirty-five, no, I'm lying, nearly thirty-seven years ago this fall. Back then it was so different around here. I tell you, you wouldn't recognize the place. There was a real sense of community, you know. Folks helped each other. Cared about each other."

She wanted to tell him to get to the point, but often, especially with lonely older people, if you gave them the chance to talk, feigned interest in their lives, they'd be far more forthcoming. "Is that so?"

"Oh yes, dear. In its day, this was a wonderful neighborhood. A place you could raise a family and know your kids were going to come home from school in one piece at the end of the day."

She nodded. "But it's not like that anymore?"

She looked at his brown wool blazer. It was buttoned up as if it was not now in the low seventies, but was a chilly autumn morning. Five would get you ten, under that jacket, he'd have a sweater vest. What was it about getting old that meant you were never warm?

He said, "You know as well as I do, the world isn't changing for the better."

"So you know most of the families around here?"

"Lived here all my life. If there's anything you need to know, I'm your man."

She held out her hand. "I'm sorry, I'm Tess Williams."

The old man tucked his walking cane under his left arm and then shook her hand, cupping it with his left hand, as if wanting to savor that tiny bit of human contact as fully as possible.

"Nathan Ridley. Everyone calls me Nat."

He smiled at her. The skin around his eyes crinkled, meaning the smile was genuine, friendly. Understanding body language helped her with her work, so little things other people might overlook she consciously analyzed. It sometimes meant the difference between knowing whether a gunman was going to pull

47

the trigger or burst into tears over what he'd done. A useful trait. But, sadly, not infallible.

She smiled back. "So did you hear anything last night, Nat?"

He rested on his cane again. "Well, I walked around the block as usual, nine p.m. I call it my patrol, but it's more a leisurely hobble with this old thing." He patted his right leg.

"Hear anything later?"

"Only when I went to the store later on. My leg was aching like nobody's business. It's rare I get a good night's sleep these days. One of the problems of getting old. Not that you'll have to worry about that for a long, long time, dear." He smiled.

"So you went out to the store and…?"

"Yes," he continued, "I figured I'd make myself a hot milky drink but I had no milk, you see. Darned if I know where it all goes." Despite his thick jacket, he rubbed his hands together. "Boy, is it me or is it a cold one today?"

There was often great value in agreeing with someone, even if you didn't hold to their viewpoint, because it helped to establish a kinship which encouraged them to open up to you.

"Yes, it is a little chilly," said Tess. "So what did you hear last night exactly?"

"If you're cold, dear, we can chat in my old place. It's only across the street." He pointed to a nearby building and a ground-level apartment.

She looked at her watch.

When he saw her hesitating, he tried to seal the deal. "I can make us some hot tea in a jiffy."

So this guy heard something last night, knew everyone in the neighborhood, and could virtually see the crime scene from his living room window.

"Tea would be lovely. Thank you."

Statistics proved most murder victims were killed by someone they knew. That meant those people who knew the victim invariably also knew the killer. Who did Nat know? Which suspects could he point her to?

Chapter 08

NAT'S APARTMENT WAS much how she'd expected it would be. When she sat on the couch the protective plastic cover squeaked and all but glued her in place, while, despite the large windows, the room's dark wood, leather, and brown furnishings made it unnaturally gloomy.

On the ebony mantel stood an arch-shaped wooden clock. It ticked louder than any clock she'd ever heard. And it seemed to tick more slowly too. As if time were tired in this house. As if it were biding time, with every day the same, just waiting for death.

"Nice place," she said, wanting to endear herself to him to get the information she needed.

He turned from pouring boiling water and smiled.

"Wouldn't live anywhere else," he said. "I know everyone and everyone knows me. It's my little plot of heaven."

She gazed about the dingy mausoleum he called home. She'd bet if he had five visitors a year, it would be a busy year.

On a five-foot table beneath the biggest window was a miniature diorama consisting of countryside dotted with tens of tiny model soldiers. Squeaking as she prized herself off the plastic, she meandered over to look while Nat was brewing tea.

"The Battle of Ball's Bluff, Virginia, 1861," he said. "I like to re-enact and study strategy."

"Uh-huh."

She studied the old man. Was he really so old and decrepit? Or did prematurely gray hair, a naturally haggard hangdog expression, and a limp make him appear far older than he actually was? It was hard to tell. He looked like he was on the wrong end of his seventies but could easily be ten or fifteen years younger.

She said, "So, you were saying you heard something late last night."

"Oh, yes. But you never said why you're here, dear. Why you were at the crime scene."

"It's part of what I do." She ambled back to the couch.

"Which is?"

She was going to have to give him something. Share so he'd do likewise.

"I write. Freelance. Sometimes I uncover things that help the police."

He hobbled over with two cups of tea on saucers. He placed them on coasters on the dark wood table in front of the couch and then sat.

Nat smiled. "So, who is it we're investigating today?"

We? So far, *we* had zip.

And the clock ticked slowly on.

"You were telling me about last night," said Tess, hoping he had more to offer than a hot drink she didn't really want.

"Oh yes. Well, it's my leg, you see. I tell you, never get old, dear. You won't believe the problems. I've got a cupboard full of pills and potions, the strongest painkillers and the most powerful sleeping pills known to man, but can I sleep? So, anyway, I decided I'd make myself a hot milky drink, see if that would do the trick, but I had no milk. So, since I wasn't doing anything else, I went to the convenience store around the block to buy some."

"Around…?"

"Just around the block, dear. You can't miss it."

"Sorry, I mean around what time."

"Oh, around two fifteen, dear. And that's when it happened."

"Yes?"

"Well, I saw young Amelia from next door having a blazing argument, first with a taxi driver and then with her boyfriend."

"Amelia? You mean Amelia Ortega?"

He gasped. "It's not Amelia, is it?" He obviously saw something in her face. "Oh dear Lord, no. Oh, the poor child."

"I'm sorry."

"Oh my. She was such a lovely girl. Led a little astray of late, but a lovely girl. Do they know who did it?"

"Not yet."

"Any clues?"

"There will be."

His expression dropped even further. "She wasn't..." He looked at the gaudy brown-and-gold-patterned carpet, no doubt a popular design three or four decades ago. He took a breath as if mustering the strength to say what he needed.

Finally, he got the words out. "She wasn't violated?"

Tess gave a slight shrug. "I'm sure the forensics team will find something to help catch the person responsible."

"Forensics, eh?" He nodded to himself. "I hope they catch them. My God, what I'd do to them if I could."

Maybe talk them to death?

"I can imagine," said Tess. "So Amelia argued with her boyfriend Ethan?"

"Yes, dear. Ethan Dumfries. They've been together around nine months."

"Did you catch what they were arguing about?"

"I'm sorry, no. I don't like to snoop."

"So how about the taxi driver? Any chance you got a good look at him?"

"Middle Eastern... maybe." He shrugged and shook his head. "I'm sorry. I'm not being much help, am I?"

"Oh, I wouldn't say that – knowing Amelia argued with someone could be crucial."

He smiled and then pulled out some scraps of paper from his sweater vest's right pocket.

"I did note the taxi's medallion number, if that's any use."

Any use? Every cab had to have a medallion to be able to pick up fares in Manhattan. Every medallion number, or cab number, was unique to a specific cab, so if she got that, she'd find the cab Amelia had taken, no problem. Thank God for busybodies and people with too much time on their hands.

He picked through the various scraps, notes scrawled on each.

"No, not that one... That one...? Nope... What's this? Oh, I mustn't lose that. Heavens, no." He looked up and smiled. "I'll have it for you in a second, dear."

She smiled.

He patted her arm. "It is so nice to have company." He went back to his notes.

Finally, he scrutinized a paper. "Hmmm... is that a five or a six? I think it's a six." He handed it to her. "There you go, dear."

6Y11.

"That's terrific. Thank you, Nat."

"My pleasure, dear. Anything to help."

"There's just one thing. Er, it might sound a little strange, but the police will be canvassing door-to-door soon. Would you mind not letting on I was here, please?"

"Well..." He scratched his head.

She knew giving people what they wanted would get her what she wanted. She laid her hand on his arm. "It would be a huge help, Nat."

He cupped her hand with his. "For you, dear." He smiled.

She stayed with Nat for another ten minutes, long enough to drink her tea and to make him feel good, useful, important, so he'd be eager to help her again should the need arise.

When she left, he waved through the security bars at his window.

She waved back. What a strange little man. Pleasant, kindly, but strange.

And deeply, deeply lonely.

Was that what was waiting for her in forty years?

That was a question for another day. Now it was time for the hunt to begin.

Chapter 09

STRIDING ALONG THE sidewalk, Tess wondered what her first move should be to find the killer.

There was absolutely no point going to Amelia's apartment as Ethan was missing. Why had he run? Either because he'd killed her or because he was afraid no one would believe he hadn't. Whichever it was, tracking him down could prove problematic.

Amelia's family? If they hadn't been involved in her death, they'd be such a mess of tears they'd be no use. On the other hand, if the family had been involved, they'd be so full of lies, it would be easier for the police to uncover the truth than for Tess to struggle with it.

Amelia's friends? Again, same problem as her family. Plus, if they did know something, and it involved a mutual friend, they may feed Tess false information out of false loyalty. She could waste hours, even days, chasing down leads only to find she was further from the truth, and the killer, than she was right now.

No, for now, her answers lay elsewhere. She needed time to formulate a plan.

A taxi having a medallion meant either it was owned by an individual, which was getting rarer nowadays since a medallion could cost hundreds of thousands of dollars, or it was one of many owned by a corporation from which drivers leased it. Either way, there'd be a record of who drove Amelia last night.

That was the good news. The bad news was that anyone could hail a yellow cab on any street, without having to go through the company's dispatcher, so to get the details of Amelia's journey would mean talking to the driver himself. That was vital anyway as Amelia had had some sort of altercation with him.

Cab drivers got irate if they didn't receive the tip they thought they deserved, so if Amelia had tried to stiff him on the fare, it could easily have led to trouble. The key could be in discovering from where she'd taken the cab and what hefty fare she'd racked up. After all, a driver wouldn't turn all Vlad the Impaler over a twenty-dollar ride, would they?

Twenty bucks? Well… People had killed for far, far less.

Once in a heightened emotional state, people did the most outrageous of things for the most ridiculous of reasons. No, she had to keep an open mind about the whole fare issue until she'd gathered more facts.

Feeling hunger gnawing at her, it approaching lunchtime, she wandered into A Taste of Napoli. She ordered a black organic tea and a small mushroom pizza, then sat at a round green table with her back to the wall and made sure she could see all the exits.

Having removed her phone from its RF shielded pouch, she scrolled through its apps until she reached Dental Schedule. That being the most boring title she could think of, she hoped if ever she lost her phone, anyone finding it would think such an app too boring to investigate. Looking directly into the camera lens on her phone, she photographed her right eye for her iris recognition software to unlock all her phone's sensitive files and features. She hadn't been able to help but feel very James Bond the first few times she'd used this security software, but these days, it was as exciting as logging in to Facebook.

Google took her to the NYC Taxi and Limousine Commission. A few clicks later, she confirmed the owner of the taxi medallion number was not an individual, but a company: Get-U-There Taxis. A trip to the dispatch office would hopefully provide the name and contact details of the driver. She continued her research.

When her order arrived, the pizza crust was chewy and the mushrooms lightly charred. She looked up at the picture of the Leaning Tower of Pisa above the counter. She sighed. That should have warned her: Pisa was a completely different town in a completely different part of Italy to Napoli, the town after which the café was named. Attention to detail was obviously not something the café's owners embraced.

Still, the tea was decent. But what kind of an imbecile would you need to be to screw up a black tea?

With music videos playing on a television suspended high on the wall toward the back of the café, she flicked through her contacts. She stopped at Bomb and hit dial, satisfied the music would mask her conversation.

Chapter 10

AFTER ONLY ONE ring, a male voice said, "Yo, Tess."

"Hey, Bomb. I need a Level Four workup on one Amelia Ortega. Priority contacts, communications for the last forty-eight hours, affiliations, images – the full gig. I'll send you the details I have. How long?"

"Corporate, government, or individual?"

"Twenty-one-year-old nobody."

"Give me an hour."

"You're going to come across Ethan Michael Dumfries. I need the same on him. Plus location updates. How long to trace his cell phone?"

"Is it turned on?"

"Don't know."

"He using Wi-Fi hotspots or a paid service?"

"Don't know."

"I'll get back to you on that when I deliver the first package."

"Great," said Tess. "How's the new housekeeper working out?"

"She didn't."

Tess sighed. That was the third in two months.

Bomb said, "Hey, she moved my keyboard. Okay?"

Hell. And she'd only been fired, not flogged? "You mean in those sixty seconds per day you pry yourself off it for a shit, shower and shave, she crept in and dusted it?"

"Funny, Tess. Real funny. As funny as if someone moves my gear and dislodges a cable, so I can't get the info you need when you need it and you end up bleeding face down in an alley."

Ah, maybe he had a point. "You could've just explained it to her."

"She got the manual. Just like all the others."

Bomb's *Housekeeper Dos and Don'ts* was indeed a 'manual' – thirty-two double-sided pages of single-spaced text. He might as well have given them the Japanese version of *War and Peace*.

She said, "Do you want me to help you find someone?"

"Thanks, but if I need help, I'll ask."

Yes, because that was what guys were renowned for – asking for help.

He said, "I'll get back to you when I have something. Ciao, Tess."

She sighed.

Just because Bomb was a genius with a computer he expected everyone else to be a genius at their chosen profession. Why couldn't he get that most people didn't pursue a calling to change the world, so much as endure a job to cover their bills? For a smart guy, he could be incredibly dumb. But hey, since when was she Little Miss Tolerance?

She left her phone out of its pouch so Bomb could reach her when he needed to. It left her susceptible to being tracked, but only if someone was actually looking for her, and looking for her at that moment. Plus, they'd need her information on the online telephone exchange Bomb had created and hidden so deep in the Deep Web, she didn't even know where it was.

She and Bomb had tried her checking in half-hourly, so her phone was only unshielded for a few minutes at a time, but it had proven unworkable. Any longer than thirty minutes would mean vital information couldn't be acted on as quickly as possible, which could mean someone ending up in the morgue – maybe her. That left only one option – the immediate job taking priority over the risk of her being tracked. It was one of the hazards of the job. Anyway, who was to say she wasn't just being paranoid?

After a couple more bites of pizza, she slung a piece of crust back onto the plate and pushed it away. Tess looked at Amelia's Facebook page on her phone.

Family rarely knew the truth about a loved one's life.

Close friends often knew more, but still had gaps in their knowledge.

Why?

Because every individual was a roiling mass of blatant contradictions, dark secrets, and impossible dreams. If you knew one person intimately over your whole lifetime, really intimately, you were truly blessed.

But secrets weren't always as safe as people liked to believe they were. Those websites people visited in the dead of night, when there was nothing around them but darkness, so they knew it was private, knew they were alone, knew they were safe... The reality was they couldn't be more vulnerable. To skilled hands, those little mouse clicks bared people's secrets as clearly as a full-page ad in the *New York Times*.

A person's true life, their true feelings, their true needs could be put together like a jigsaw puzzle if you just had enough pieces. Did they surf any unusual websites? Who were their most messaged contacts? Which groups did they look at but not join? What forum questions did they read? Which words did they google? Yes, if you knew how to mine for data, and how to recognize patterns, a person's online history could give a truer picture of their life than their parents, partner, and friends combined.

Luckily for Tess, Bomb was a jigsaw genius.

She left the café and found the nearest subway station. Moments later, she was rocketing through the bowels of the city towards the most brutal killer she'd ever encountered.

She hoped.

The Thompson job had been exhausting. Mentally and physically. It would be great if she could end this job quickly and get some time to relax, away from a world of endless exploitation and savagery. Even if just for a few days.

And that looked like a distinct possibility, with only three suspects: Ethan, who'd done it in a jealous rage; the cab driver, who'd done it after an argument had escalated; a third, as yet unidentified, individual, who'd done it because they were a psychopath looking for media attention, which was obvious by the way Amelia's body had been displayed.

Lover, driver, psycho. Which one would it be?

Chapter 11

LIVING IN NEW York City was like living in a land where everyone and anyone could be a cannibal looking for their next meal – in public, no one made eye contact in case that one person you connected with had polished their silverware that very morning.

Obviously unaware it was supposed to be invisible on the subway train, an auburn-haired baby didn't see anything wrong in bawling, making itself the center of attention. The center of attention for all but its mother. Looking over the top of it at her ereader, she gently rocked her child, but paid no heed to the fact that her maternal efforts were achieving absolutely squat.

The kid wailed. And wailed. And wailed.

Christ, Tess hated that sound. And she hated that kind of parent – they never seemed to give a crap about how many people their kid irritated as they blissfully went about their lives. Despite her meditation practices, this was one of those noises she just couldn't tune out. Which made it even more irritating.

The kid's scream turned into a guttural squeal, but still the mother was oblivious.

God only knew why there weren't laws against traveling with kids under five years old. Especially in such confined areas as trains and planes. Oh, man... planes. On her flight to Shanghai, she'd had to ask the old guy next to her for one of his sleeping pills because of the spawn of Satan wailing in the seat behind her. It was either that or risk killing every passenger onboard by opening the emergency hatch to pitch the squealing brat into the clouds.

The flight attendant had suggested Tess couldn't ignore the baby's distress cries because of her maternal instincts. After Tess had stopped laughing, she'd given the idea some consideration. And then burst out laughing again.

Maternal? Yeah, she was as maternal as a great white shark with a seal pup.

Back in the daylight on the street, surrounded by the serene cacophony of the city's honking, revving, bustling life, Tess strolled into Get-U-There Taxis. It was only a small company, so she hoped she wouldn't have much trouble getting the information she needed.

With the stench of gas and oil hanging heavy in the air, she stepped over a soggy black patch on the concrete floor and headed for what looked like the office. In the doorway stood a scrawny man with a moustache that jutted out from his face as far as his nose.

As she marched over, Moustache Man eyed her head to toe.

She couldn't have hoped for anything better – a horny guy well below her league. She smiled at him.

He smiled back. "Can I help you, miss?"

"Hi. I'm looking for a driver."

"And where do you wanna go?"

"I'd like to know who was driving cab 6Y11 between midnight and five a.m., please." The time of death estimate and Nat's memory could both have been inaccurate, so best to play safe with a wide time frame.

"Ah, see, we don't give information like that to members of the public."

She glanced to the back of the garage, where two cabs had their hoods up but no one working on them while a third stood on blocks.

She looked back at the mustachioed dispatcher. On the front of his white shirt he'd sponged a ketchup stain to save wasting a fresh garment when there was still wear in that one.

When a taxi medallion could cost upwards of a million bucks, any company that didn't have its fleet on the road 24/7 was a failing company. This was a guy going nowhere in a company on the ropes.

She smiled. "Fifty bucks for a name."

"If it's worth fifty, it must be worth a hundred." He smiled. Smiled like he knew the game they were playing and how he could win.

He didn't.

She said, "It's worth forty-five. Or I walk."

"You said fifty."

"Now it's forty."

"Okay, okay." He threw his hands up and trudged into the office. "Jesus. A guy's gotta make a living, you know." He leaned over his desk and hit a couple of keys on his keyboard. "Yeah, it's Amir Suleman."

Tess spelled the name out to check she'd gotten it right, then said, "And where will I find Mr. Suleman?"

Moustache Man folded his arms, put on a stern expression, and then held out a hand, rubbing his thumb over his fingertips for the money. This was his idea of hardball? Awww, bless his heart.

Tess handed him forty dollars.

"This time of day, he'll be at the corner of Baker and Richmond. Look for Eastern Promise food truck. He's working two jobs since his wife took the house and most of his paycheck."

Money. As was so often the case, was money at the root of this crime?

Getting stiffed on a fare wouldn't directly lead a cab driver to impale a woman on a metal pole. No, but one person in effect stealing from another invariably led to a verbal attack, which invariably led to a physical assault, which invariably led to one hell of an escalation where rationality disappeared and all that mattered was payback. In the eyes of the person who'd been wronged, the sum in question became inconsequential. It could be twenty dollars as easily as twenty thousand. Now, it was all about payback. Payback at any cost.

Could Amir have killed Amelia over less than the average Joe would pay for a decent pizza?

Chapter 12

SITTING ON A fire hydrant outside Manning's Bikes, Tess looked over at the bright green food truck with 'Eastern Promise' emblazoned across it in black and gold letters. Fifty yards diagonally across from her, a couple of customers waited for food. The lunchtime rush ending, she'd wait a few more minutes until Amir was doing nothing but wiping down his counter. Make her approach in private.

Tess returned to browsing files on her phone.

She read through another of Amelia's private Facebook messages that Bomb had emailed her. So far, there was nothing concrete to suggest any lover except Ethan. Neither did her Internet browsing reveal any gang-related talk, sexual deviancy, or Internet dating – any of which could have led her into a dangerous situation.

In green Kawasaki leathers, a biker grinned at Tess on the hydrant. "You're sitting in the wrong place, baby, if you want something big and hard between your legs." Grabbing his crotch, he nudged his black-clad friend. They both laughed.

She ignored them. Banter would lead nowhere and confrontation would alert Amir to her abilities. She returned to her files.

To a female friend called Becks, Amelia made occasional references to TG, as though it was someone's name. As Tess trawled back through the messages to find where this story started, she found multiple references first to 'that guy' and then further back to 'that guy in the bar'. Had 'that guy in the bar' morphed into 'that guy' and then into simply 'TG'? Without giving details, the texts referred to something Amelia had done, innumerable times and in a variety of public places, which she didn't want Ethan to discover. Was TG a nameless fuck buddy Amelia sometimes ran into? Did she revel in an element of danger? If so, exactly how much danger did she enjoy?

Unfortunately, there'd been no direct communication with TG and no photo. Amelia was probably wary of Ethan gaining access to her account and seeing something incriminating. Finding TG was going to be a problem. A bar at which they'd regularly met, however, was mentioned.

Shades.

Another phrase also captured Tess's attention. A month ago, Amelia had made a 'huge mistake' after TG had finally said he loved her. Amelia's messages concerning him had become much darker after that. There was far less hope. Far less sense of fulfillment in the danger. Far less sparkle.

What had Amelia done that was such a 'huge mistake'? Or, more likely, what had TG made her do? And what had that incident led to? Was TG that third unidentified suspect – the psychopath? Had he turned into a jealous lover? Or had Ethan discovered Amelia's secret and sought to punish her for her betrayal?

Tess needed answers.

She looked up. A lone customer was being served at the truck. Time to grill a taxi-driving chef.

Chapter 13

AMIR SULEMAN, THE taxi driver, looked down at her through the hatch in the side of his green truck. "What I can do for you?"

From his accent, his dark skin, and the name of his food truck, Tess guessed he was from the Middle East. Lebanon, Syria, maybe Turkey.

"Your chili special – is that hot?"

"Is hot."

She smiled. "I love hot."

"Is very hot."

"Can I get four portions? To take home, please?"

"Will take a few minutes."

"That's okay." She watched him put a large saucepan of chili on his stove and turn up the heat. "This an old family recipe?"

He didn't turn. "No."

"Is it Turkish?"

"No."

She sighed. Talk about hard work. Finesse would obviously not win this battle.

"You're a taxi driver, aren't you?"

He still didn't turn from cooking. "Yes."

"Could you tell me about one of your fares last night?"

He stopped what he was doing and turned. Holding a large knife, he said, "Police?"

"No."

"Then I say nothing." He turned back to his cocking.

"You picked up a young woman. Slim. Twenty-one. You dropped her—"

He turned around again, gesturing with the knife. "You don't speak English? I say 'I say nothing.' Now you go. I don't cook for you."

"She was killed last night."

His mouth dropped open. His eyes glazed for a moment while he processed the information. Then he stabbed his knife towards her. "And you think I did it?"

"I need to know what you know."

"I know nothing without lawyer." He stabbed his knife down the street. "You go."

She looked at the middle-aged man before her. Looked at his greasy hair, the dark rings under his eyes, his slumped shoulders. Life hadn't been good to this man. Whether that was deserved or not didn't matter. What mattered was such a man would grasp any chance to feel, even for the most fleeting of moments, like a winner.

She slammed banknotes down on his counter. "I've got fifty bucks… or a warm, soft mouth."

Her gaze fell to his crotch.

73

Chapter 14

GOING DOWN ONTO her knees in the food truck, Tess's hand stuck to the greasy floor. No way had a health inspector visited this thing recently. God only knew what she'd catch if she didn't wash her hands after this.

She peeled her palm off the floor, snagged a couple of paper napkins from a shelf under the counter, and wiped her hands. She looked up at Amir Suleman towering over her. He double-checked the shutters over the truck's serving hatch were locked. And then unzipped his pants.

Thank God he'd picked this option. She was struggling to make all her rent payments this month as it was, so she couldn't afford to blow too much of this week's budget on bribes.

Using both hands, she eased out his pecker.

The smell hit her instantly. A smell most women have encountered and each dreads encountering again – like rotting meat a dog has pissed on. It was no wonder his wife left him. Such a smell alone was tantamount to domestic abuse.

That was the bad news.

But there was good news – it wasn't the biggest dick she'd ever had to cope with, so it wouldn't give her jaw-ache. And despite the smell, it did look clean.

She took him into her mouth and sucked.

What was it about men and personal hygiene? Hell, most guys took better care of their car than their pecker: they wouldn't stick their beloved vehicle in any old place but only in places they knew and trusted; they were obsessive about having it not just in functional condition, but as impressive as possible; they were particular about who even touched it let alone drove it. But their pecker? An actual piece of their own body? Hey, who cared what sleazy neighborhood that had to venture into and who got their hands on it?

Where was the logic?

Still, who was she to talk? She'd had worse things than a grimy dick in her mouth – living and dead, and cooked and raw. The worst must have been China. Their markets stocked packets of frozen dog meat, deep-fried starfish on a stick, snake skin – not snake meat, that was another dish entirely, but just the skin. How the devil could you make a meal out of skin?

Amir making guttural moaning sounds, she wondered if passers-by could hear. So what if they could – they weren't her customers.

To speed things along, she got to work with her hand.

Scorpions, wild birds, insects… The Chinese diet seemed to leave no species off the menu.

Oh, seahorses!

That had to be the worst 'food source' she'd found there.

As respite from her brutal training regiment, she'd spent many an hour sitting on the floor of Shanghai Ocean Aquarium, basking in the gentle world of the seahorses as they glided about their tank. Outside, only a leisurely stroll away, grilled seahorse was on sale at a local food market. How could the Chinese do that? Marvel at a creature one minute, then slap it on their dinner plate the next? And seahorses truly were wondrous. Such beautiful, peaceful little creat—

Amir groaned. He grabbed the counter edge to steady himself.

Something hit the back of her throat.

Pulling away, she flung her free hand over the end of his pecker and caught the rest of his gunk in a clean napkin. She continued pumping with her other hand to empty him into the tissue paper.

Feeling him softening, she let go and looked up, nodding to the napkin. "Don't want the health inspector shutting you down, do we?"

She knew she should feel some sort of revulsion over what she'd just done, or guilt, or shame, but she didn't. She didn't have the money to buy what she wanted so she'd traded what she did have for it. It was a simple transaction. Nothing more. Sex could get her pretty much anything she wanted – the favors she got from her many cop fuck buddies was proof of that.

Maybe it would be different if she enjoyed sex. Or if she was in a relationship. But she didn't and she wasn't. So why not use sex as a simple commodity? When other people prized it so highly, that gave her an instant advantage.

Amir distracted, dressing himself, she stuffed the napkin into her pocket and then swiped a can of cola from a storage shelf. "I'm sure you won't mind."

She took a good swig and swished it around her mouth, but grimaced. "Urgh… warm."

She looked at Amir, "Now, about last night."

"I think… I wait for lawyer."

Chapter 15

TESS JABBED HER cola at him. "Hey, whoa there, cowboy. We had a deal."

"Deals change. Here, I give you free chili." He moved toward his saucepan, still on the stove beside her.

"Like hell." She pushed him back. "You're going to tell me what I want to know. Now do you want to do it standing up smiling, or lying on the floor bleeding?"

He laughed. "You threaten me?" He pointed at her. "You?"

She grabbed his finger and bent it back toward him.

He winced.

She bent further.

To stop his finger from breaking, Amir bent his knees and leaned backwards.

With her foot, Tess swept his feet from under him.

He crashed to the floor.

"Just remember: I tried to play nice." She whipped the saucepan of simmering chili from the stove. Threw it into his lap. With her foot, she held the upended saucepan on him.

Amir screamed, the boiling chili soaking through his clothes onto his crotch.

She said, "Tell me what happened and I'll move my foot."

He grabbed the pan, obviously thinking he could pull it away, but cried out and pulled his hands away instead, the pan was so hot. He wrung his hands in the air.

"Tell me!"

In between gasps, he said, "Her boyfriend." His face screwed up in pain. "They fight."

"And?"

"An old man."

"What about an old man?"

"They fight also."

"She had an argument with an old man?"

"Yes. Yes. Yes." He whimpered. "Now, please."

Tess pressed down with her foot on the pan. "When you've told me everything."

Amir let out a gargling cry. He said, "Old man with stick. Old man with stick."

Nat? Surely he couldn't mean Nat.

She said, "And then what?"

"She went to store. She buy something. She leave."

"But why were you at the store? Why didn't you leave after you dropped her?"

"I buy cigarettes; I smoke cigarette."

"You didn't see the boyfriend or old man again?"

"No." His face twisted with pain and despair. "Please, please, I beg you!"

She kicked the saucepan away. He curled over. Grabbed his crotch. Whimpered.

So that was why he didn't want to confess to seeing Amelia later – other than the killer, he was likely the last person to see her alive. People had witnessed him argue with her and threaten her, so who could blame him for withholding information to avoid a lot or sweaty hours under police interrogation?

Tess turned to leave, but huffed. She stamped her foot into the floor a few times to test it, then bent her leg to see the underneath of the sneaker that had held the boiling hot pan on Amir. A crescent shaped groove from the saucepan's base had melted into the sole throwing out the balance when she stood on it.

"Oh, for God's sake." She glared at him. "Would you look at what you've done?"

She looked around. "Well, don't think this is coming out of my pocket." She hit No Sale on his cash register and snatched seventy dollars.

As she opened the door at the back of the truck to leave, she turned.

Still curled on the floor, Amir splashed a bottle of spring water over his crotch. He sobbed.

Tess shook her head. "Think that's pain? Try getting a Brazilian with hot wax. Pussy." She slammed the door behind her.

Back on the street, Tess placed the soiled napkin in a plastic bag and into her backpack. You never knew when DNA evidence could come in handy.

Heading toward the subway, she wondered why Nat hadn't told her he'd had a run-in with Amelia. What was he hiding? And, more to the point, what could they have argued about? He was boring, yes. But if that were a crime, the majority of the population would be behind bars. Apart from that, and though she didn't like to admit it even only to herself, she actually quite liked the guy.

She liked his understated control, his meekness, his concern for those around him, his inherent goodness. While each passing year colored her memories more, and there had been more years than she cared to remember, she could see her deceased grandpa in Nat.

Oh, her grandpa hadn't been boring, but he'd been soft-spoken, polite, had interests that both insulated and isolated him from other people.

Yes, maybe that was why she liked the little old man.

But why would anyone fight with Nat? He was what he was – an absent-minded, lonely old man. Pleasant, polite… harmless.

Or was he?

Around the dinner table, some of history's most notorious killers had been charming and entertaining.

Every single person had at least one secret. A secret they ached to take to the grave. What was Nat's?

Chapter 16

AS TESS DESCENDED the narrow subway steps, people bustled left and right, each lost in their own little world of importance, dreams and fears.

Equally distracted, Tess drifted down the steps. She couldn't help but wonder about Nat. Did he harbor a dark secret or was he just the amiable, if pitiable, figure he appeared? More crucially, why was she struggling to tell which was the case? She could usually read people well. Was his similarity to her grandpa coloring her judgment? She needed answers. Needed clarity.

Halfway down the steps, her phone rang. "I hope this is good news, Bomb."

"I think I'm homing in on our boy Ethan. Unless something changes, I should have a location sometime within the next hour. Ninety minutes max."

"Great. Thanks, Bomb."

"Good hunting. Ciao, Tess."

She climbed back up the steps and marched along the street toward a bus stop she'd spotted. If Bomb could call anytime within the next ninety minutes, she couldn't get caught deep underground with no cell phone signal, miss his call, and thus miss Ethan because she reached his location too late.

To be better able to discuss options with him, she'd once asked Bomb to explain how he did what he did. She'd even started recording the session to review the more technical aspects later.

Review the more 'technical' aspects? Who was she fooling?

Aside from the software he'd coded himself, it was all to do with Google dorks, open ports, shellcode, brute force password crackers, IP addresses, Skipfish, ZAP, trojans, worms, Burp, bots, and backdoors. Talk about hi-tech wizardry only a NASA scientist could appreciate.

Luckily, her battery had died, so they'd had to stop long before he'd run out of details or enthusiasm.

If he'd lived in Silicon Valley in the 80s, he'd have been hailed as a genius. But born a decade too late and three thousand miles away in a rundown apartment building controlled by a loan shark, Bomb hadn't been blessed by serendipity.

But fate had a weird way of choosing your path at times. As she knew only too well. You could do all you could to make the right decisions, but sometimes, even in hindsight, you could never see how you could've done anything differently for things to have turned out any better. But then, wasn't that what made life so interesting? A utopia would be fun. For a while. But if there were no more challenges? Well, humanity would just fade away. Die of boredom.

Yeah, there was something to be said for hardship. It pushed you. Made you work for what you wanted. Made you resourceful. Made you better. Stronger. Most of the time.

Other times, it twisted you into a perverse image of humanity. Doing to a person's soul what a Hall of Mirrors did to their body – warping and corrupting, turning the beautiful into something hideous.

It was a fine line between being a good person and a bad one. Between hero and monster. A fine line that every single person had to choose, all by themselves, on which side they wanted to stand. It was easy to be a hero – you just chose to do good things.

The problem was it was even easier to be a monster.

Put your toe just a fraction of an inch too far over the line... and there you were: cheating on your partner; skimming off a few dollars from your boss's takings; backstabbing your friend for a promotion. Little things. Yes. But little things were never enough. Not once you'd started. Not once you'd seen how ridiculously easy it was. And that was when the monster inside everyone came a-calling.

The strange thing was, the slide from hero to monster was so, so easy. Yet the climb back from monster to hero? Like climbing Mount Everest. And she should know.

En route to Nat's, Tess received the full workup on Ethan, so she took a minor detour. Examining multiple files on her phone wasn't fun, because, ideally, you needed to have as many open as possible to make cross-referencing easier. Her tablet was okay, but with two Level 4 workups, a full-size screen was the best option.

In school, while the other kids had all been dreaming of being a wizard learning magic in a mystical castle, she'd dreamed of being a librarian. With thousands and thousands of books at your fingertips, every day all day, what more could anyone possibly want?

Like an ancient queen entering the temple to her gods, Tess climbed the stone steps to the white marble building fronted by grand porticos and Corinthian columns – the public library. She glanced at the huge marble lions on either side, Fortitude and Patience, guarding the entrance. No matter how many times she came here, it always filled her with wonder.

For her, as a small child, this had been a magic castle. Or as near to a castle as she'd ever seen. It had been her favorite place in the whole city. The Statue of Liberty, the Bronx Zoo, the view from the top of the Twin Towers... All too small. Too limiting. Too unadventurous. The library, on the other hand, housed the whole world – and how she'd globetrotted.

Stories from every age, country and culture. Facts from every discipline, hobby and sport. Wisdom from every thinker, religion and philosophy. She'd devoured it all.

And thank God. If it hadn't been for her appreciation of books, appreciation of learning, appreciation of how others had faced impossible odds yet triumphed, the path her life had taken would surely have seen her as a junkie stealing to numb her pain. Or a suicide victim. Both of which pretty much amounted to the same thing.

Sitting at a wide wooden desk in the third-floor Catalogue Room, beneath one of the four-tier circular chandeliers, Tess fired up one of the computers. After inserting her USB drive to have available the array of apps Bomb had created for her, she logged in to Bomb's darknet.

Using AES-Twofish-Serpent cascaded three-cipher encryption, Eastern European servers, and domains registered in the Far East, Bomb had created a website Tess could access on the move while making it virtually impervious to detection. 'Virtually impervious' – as with everything online, it was a trade-off between security and functionality.

She followed Bomb's instructions to establish backdoor access to both Amelia's and Ethan's social media and email accounts. Going in through a backdoor meant, firstly, the police wouldn't be suspicious about a dead girl accessing her account and, secondly, that Ethan wouldn't be frozen out and, therefore, suspicious by there being two simultaneous logins to his accounts. More importantly, it meant no one would be able to track Tess's cyberspace movements.

Bomb's software had already completed basic pattern recognition and cross-referencing of the accounts for names, places, dates and other preprogrammed criteria within set parameters, so Tess began digging.

From the photos she'd seen on her phone, she'd already memorized Ethan's face, but a larger screen meant she could see more detail. Now, she saw a crescent-shaped scar on the left side of his jaw that she hadn't earlier – an excellent unique identifier. At least now, whether she saw him in a bar or on a mortuary slab, she'd know he was the guy she was looking for.

Or one of them. How about TG?

There was no such reference in any of Ethan's online messages.

His phone records, however, proved far more interesting. After an initial phone call that morning which had lasted just one minute forty-seven seconds, Ethan had bombarded Amelia's friend Becks with messages.

Tess counted the entries: twelve phone calls and twenty-seven texts. He'd tried to contact her more than three times as often as any of Amelia's other friends.

Opening the attachment sent with one message, Tess found a shadowy photo of a woman talking intimately to a man at a bar. The woman looked like Amelia, while the club could've been Shades, which Ethan referenced elsewhere. As for the man? Could that be the elusive TG?

The message with the photo simply said, *'tell me who so i can kill him.'*

Tess zoomed in to the photo for a better look at TG, but with a low-resolution image taken in a dark club, his face was just a shadowy, pixelated mess. She ran the photo through their site's image-enhancement software. It reduced the number of artifacts, but, with the source image of such low quality, the face was little but a blurry oval blob. She'd never identify TG with this.

Other than the first, all Ethan's calls to Becks had gone unanswered; most of the texts had gone unread.

Hardly surprising. Most contained threats. All very blunt. All very graphic.

Ethan sounded like an incredibly nice guy. Tess couldn't wait to meet him.

One phrase was common to many of his messages: *'i didnt do it.'*

Becks had only sent one SMS reply: *'I DON'T BELIEVE U!!!'*

At the crime scene, Mac had said Ethan had a record of violence against women. Becks obviously knew he was a violent man, while his messages gave every indication he saw violence as an acceptable solution to his problems. It was easy to see how a fight with Amelia might have got out of hand.

But why was he so desperate to talk with Becks? Did he want her to provide an alibi for the time of the murder? Did he think she knew he'd abused Amelia and was worried she'd tell the police? Was he innocent and simply trying to trace the man in the photo talking to Amelia, either to clear his name, or to seek vengeance, believing this stranger to be the killer?

As Tess scanned the texts for more clues, Bomb posted Ethan's latest message to Becks. It left little doubt about his intentions: *'tell me who it is or after i've found him i'll find u.'*

Tess checked Becks's profile: she waited tables at A Taste of Napoli, where Tess had eaten earlier. A black woman with straightened shoulder-length hair and a smoldering look, all Becks's photos screamed 'sassy'. She and Amelia obviously had an active social life and appeared to share everything. Maybe Becks held the key. Scanning through the photos Becks had uploaded to her Facebook account, Tess came to a number of interesting ones. She sent them to her phone just as it vibrated.

Gesturing to the librarian that she'd be back after taking a call, Tess removed her USB drive and then ducked out. She strode through the immense Reading Room as quickly as she could and into the McGraw Rotunda, a 'hallway' more suited to a European palace than a city public library.

Surrounded by French walnut and pink marble, and beneath a gigantic ceiling mural of Prometheus stealing fire from the Gods, Tess answered her phone.

"I located your boy," said Bomb.

"Great. How close is he?"

"He's on the move. Has been for an hour now. Seems to be just hopping on and off the public transit system. Probably thinks if he keeps moving no one will find him."

"Let me know when he stops in one place for longer than twenty minutes. Or if you find a pattern."

"You got it."

"Thanks, Bomb." She hung up.

There was no point in trying to chase Ethan around the city. If he was taking random routes, it was impossible to guess where he was going to be at any one time. But if it was random, he wouldn't sit tight for more than a few minutes, but just take the first bus or train that came along. If he stopped for twenty minutes, it was a fair bet he'd reached where he wanted to be and would be there for much longer.

They say a criminal often returns to the scene of a crime. The dumb ones, yes. Or the really smart ones who believe they can throw a wrench in the works for the investigators. Most, however, just run. Was Ethan running because he had something to hide? Or running because he had someone to find? And if the latter, what would he do when he found them? If he wasn't guilty of murder now, would he be guilty come morning?

Tess phoned A Taste of Napoli and asked for Becks. The man who answered said she was busy with a customer so asked if Tess could hold a moment. "That's okay. I'll send her a text. Thanks."

The phone call being simple enough not to arouse suspicion, Tess returned to the computer and gathered up her belongings. Becks was at the restaurant. She'd be distraught about the death of her best friend, but probably felt safe surrounded by other people, so she wouldn't be rushing to go home.

Ethan had ceaselessly denied any involvement in Amelia's death, but what else would anyone expect of a murder suspect? He had also endlessly demanded the name of the man Amelia had been with in Shades. And constantly threatened untold violence. He needed stopping. But to stop him, Tess needed answers.

And then there was what Amelia had called her 'huge mistake.' What was that and had it led to her death?

This sordid little saga was like some cheap daytime soap opera. Except, in this one, no amount of imaginative scriptwriting would bring the heroine back from beyond the grave.

With the early evening's shadows creeping across Fifth Avenue, forewarning of the imminent demise of another day, Tess left the library and strode toward the subway station at the far side of Bryant Park.

Enjoying the last of the day's sun, New Yorkers lounged with friends on rickety green metal chairs scattered along the tree-lined South Promenade.

At the intersection of two paths, beneath a towering London plane tree, a black guy in grubby denims played saxophone. Eyes shut and seeming not to care whether anyone was listening or not, he swayed to the music of his own private world.

All around, people chatted and laughed and smiled and chilled.

Meandering through them, Tess couldn't help but notice one glaring thing – they all made it look as if life was so easy.

If only.

But then, she'd chosen her lifestyle. And while her work might be as difficult as it was dangerous, no job she took was ever impossible. Someone always knew something. Always. The secret was in finding them.

With no way to identify TG or to locate Ethan, Tess had one choice, one slender hope: find Becks. Amelia's best friend would know the full story on Ethan and TG, and as she was being threatened herself, would be eager to help anyone who could protect her. Hopefully. The theory was logical, but unfortunately, people invariably weren't.

Becks was the key. Tess was sure. But was there something else? Something vital she was overlooking?

Tess's mind lost, struggling for answers to impossible questions, she drifted through her fellow New Yorkers.

A chubby power-walker panted her way up the path toward Tess. Red-faced and puffing as if she was running the New York Marathon, not merely ambling around a football-field-sized lawn, she glared at Tess for being in her direct path, despite there being ample room to pass on either side.

Tess barely registered it. She couldn't shake the feeling she'd missed something.

Like straining to reach a pen on the floor only for it to flick away under the pressure of her fingertip, a thought lay just out of reach of her grasping mind, both there and not there.

What the devil was it? Or was she just imagining it?

Having exited the park, Tess descended the subway steps on Sixth Avenue, still lost in thought.

People bustled all around her. Workers, shoppers, tourists, daydreamers, moochers… Everyone seemed to know exactly what they were doing and where they were going. It was as if they were all privy to some grand plan.

Everyone but her.

She had an idea for what to do next, yes, but something felt... felt off.

As they passed, someone bumped Tess's shoulder.

It didn't hurt.

Didn't even throw her off her stride.

But she gasped.

Tensed.

A chill scraped down her spine as if someone had dragged a dagger made of ice across her bare flesh.

She grabbed the metal handrail. Gripped it tight.

"Oh, Jesus." That was him!

She was sure of it.

Him!

Chapter 17

IT HAD BEEN seventeen years since she'd last seen *him*, but she was sure the guy who'd just bumped into her was the killer who'd ruined her life when she was just a child. She'd only caught a glimpse of him today, but it had been so much closer than those other times.

She clutched her chest, her heart pounding so hard it felt like it might burst out at any second.

Oh, God, it really was *him.*

The blood drained from her face just as the energy drained from her body. Hyperventilating, she clung to the cold metal rail, confused thoughts skittering through her mind.

With her legs shaking like those of a newborn lamb, she gripped the rail so hard her knuckles whitened as she desperately tried to steady herself.

It was him. She was certain.

Wasn't she?

Of course she was. How could she ever forget *him!*

She dragged a trembling hand over her brow. Realized it was shaking. Stared at it.

Calmness. She needed calmness. If she intended to face the sadistic killer she'd just seen, she needed total focus. Any other state would and she'd be the one lying motionless in a pool of blood.

Forcing her breathing to slow and deepen, she felt air flowing into her and expanding, then radiating through her like the glow of the sun on a blissful summer's morning. A calmness gradually swept over her, a calmness that gave her mastery of her thoughts, her body, her life.

After a few moments, she again held her hand up before her. Rock steady.

She spun. Scrambled back up the steps to the street. Stared through the crowd for the man she hadn't seen for seventeen years, the man who'd ruined her life by robbing her of her family.

Where was he?

Wriggling her way through the people swarming toward the subway, she scanned for the killer.

Where the devil was he?

She spun. Stared. Spun again. Scoured the packed street and the sea of faces. So many faces. But not the one she wanted. Again, her heart started hammering as if someone long dead had just breezed past her.

Where the—

There!

Way ahead, an average-height man in a black hoodie meandered down the sidewalk. Him!

Though she couldn't see his face, that was the same man who'd just bumped into her. No mistake. That was her target.

Adrenaline shook her body with nervous energy.

Finally, after seventeen years, she had him.

Tess stormed along the crowded sidewalk.

She'd always known this was how it would go down – just a chance encounter when she least expected it. But here? Right now...?

She'd waited for seventeen years. Prepared for seventeen years. Yet fear and anxiety swamped her system. Even after all that time, she wasn't ready. But it wasn't like she had any other choice but to grab this chance.

A skinny woman with shopping bags in either hand dawdled along the busy street. Tess barged by her, knocking her into a display of magazines outside a newsstand.

Two chubby guys in suits waddled toward Tess, laughing about God only knew what, but taking up way too much of the sidewalk. She crashed straight through the middle of them.

She didn't see any of the angry glares.

Didn't hear any of the angry words.

Her world consisted of one thing and only one thing: him.

Like a salmon fighting its way back upstream to find the point at which it had been spawned, Tess fought through the swarming pedestrians to reach the man who had turned her world into a nightmare and set her on the path to being the killer she was today – the monster who had created her.

Weaving in and out of the surging wave of people, she struggled to fix her gaze on him as endless bodies seemed to delight in blocking her path, as if determined to hide him and to cheat her out of her justice.

Again, she lost sight of him.

And again, she agonizingly scoured the sea of faces.

Where was he? Where the hell was he? Where—

There!

Tess ripped her backpack off her back as she tore through the crowd. She was not geared up for combat, but if she caught him by surprise, that wouldn't be too much of a problem. Still, having witnessed his brutality, she needed an edge if she was going to tackle him out in the open. Especially if she hoped to do it so fast that she could be little but a blur in the crowd and thus get away with it.

She whipped out her armored black leather gloves. With her eyes fixed on the man sauntering along some distance ahead as if he didn't have a care in the world, she pulled on the left one. The one-tenth-of-an-inch-thick titanium alloy plates cocooned her hand in metal – a lethal gauntlet for the twenty-first century. But with her gaze nailed to the man, as she bustled past a woman pushing a stroller, she dropped her right glove.

"Goddamnit." She bent to snatch it up. A teenager in jeans dashed by and kicked it.

Tess scrambled back along the pavement. She thrust out her hand just as some guy glued to his phone was about to step on her glove. The guy's peripheral vision must have caught her, because he sidestepped without even looking up.

Tess grabbed her glove. Yanked it on. Spun. Stared ahead.

The killer had disappeared.

She tore back through the hordes of pedestrians, clawing her way through the meandering wall of flesh. Frantically, she scoured further up the sidewalk.

He had to be there. Had to be.

But there was no sign.

This couldn't happen. She couldn't get so close and then lose him. No. Please, no. Not again.

She battled against the river of bodies rushing down the sidewalk, desperate to sweep her up and carry her away in completely the wrong direction, carry her away into despair and loss and darkness.

She wove and twisted and barged and…

Her eyes popped wide and she gasped.

There!

Barely twenty yards ahead, the killer nonchalantly waltzed into a department store.

Tess scrambled straight through the middle of a family of burger lovers who enveloped the entire sidewalk from side to side. She raced after him.

She had him. She goddamn had him.

Tess flew to the entrance. She glared up at the electronic sensor as the doors crawled apart with all the speed of a glacier. As Tess tried to squeeze through before the doors had fully opened, a chubby woman blocked her way, appearing to be arguing with a balding man over how much she'd just paid for some scent.

"Excuse me." Tess tried to squeeze between them.

"Do you mind!" The woman glared at Tess and shifted to purposefully obstruct her all the more. "Can't you see we're having a conversation here?"

"And can't you see you're blocking the fucking doorway?"

Tess barged through and into the store.

Women sniffed fragrances on their wrists, clerks smiled with lips so glossy it was as if they applied fresh lipstick every few seconds, cash registers chinged and card readers beeped.

Tess pulled up. Gasping for breath. Even though she could run a mile and barely break a sweat, her mind had sent her body into overdrive. Gulping air, she wiped her brow and peered across the huge sales area.

Tess's gaze shot from one side of the room to the other, one perfume counter to the other, one face to another.

He was here. He was here. He was here. She'd seen him. But where?

A pudgy security guard sporting a bushy moustache plodded over.

"Are you okay, miss?"

She barely noticed anyone had said anything.

There he was!

Tess sped along the main aisle toward the inner depths of the store and a section dedicated to male cosmetics and grooming.

She had him. She goddamn had him.

And hell, was he going to bleed.

Tess hurtled by a woman at one of the display counters and knocked a glass bottle from her hands. It crashed down onto a display, sending other bottles flying. The woman shouted something, but Tess was already past her and way too close to the killer to care.

She had him.

Two young girls ambled along, laughing and smelling a new scent they'd bought. Tess barged between them.

She flew through the store.

Then...

She was there. Only ten feet from the man who'd destroyed everything she'd loved.

With his back to her, he stared at a display of electric shavers. As he perused the rows of products, he turned, which allowed anyone behind him to see part of his face.

Tess caught her breath.

It was him. *It was him!*

She trembled with nervous energy. She'd dreamed of this moment for so long. Dreamed of it. Ached for it. Prayed for it.

And now it was here.

Finally, the man who'd ruined her life was going to die. In a surprise attack like this, she'd need only a few seconds, then she'd run like hell and go to ground. Or escape on a plane back to China. Or end up in Sing Sing. It didn't matter. All that mattered was that she'd finally found him.

The man held up one of the shavers and said something to the immaculately groomed male clerk. They both laughed.

Tess sneered. He had no idea that that was the very last thing he was ever going to say.

She stared at him.

All she had to do was reach out.

Reach out and end the nightmare.

End it by ending him.

Chapter 18

THE CLERK BEHIND the male grooming counter eyed Tess warily.

And the killer noticed it.

He turned.

Tess had suffered for seventeen torturously long years. But the nightmare was going to end, because she was going to have her justice. Right this second.

She surged forward.

Knocked the killer over backwards so he sprawled on his back over the counter.

Pulled her fist back to hammer into his throat and pound the life out of him that very instant.

She ached to see his blood. Ached to hear his screams. Ached to know true justice.

But she gasped. Froze.

The face staring back at her, with mouth agape and eyes wide with fear, was not *his* face.

The same kind of high cheekbones, yes. The same jawline. The same pointed nose. The same eyes. Just not *him*.

The man threw his hands up and twisted away, cowering from the impending beating.

Tess let go of him and staggered back, holding her hands up submissively.

"It's okay. I..." She slumped, completely exhausted. "I—I thought you were someone else."

"Asshole." He glowered at her as he pushed off the counter.

Panting as if she'd been sprinting all day, she said, "I'm so sorry. Really. I honestly th—"

Hands grabbed Tess from behind.

The pudgy mustachioed security guard and a gray-haired colleague pinned her arms and bundled her further back from the innocent man.

Pudgy Guard said, "Are you okay, sir? Would you like us to call the police so you can press charges?"

Tess fell limp. Let the guards restrain her, even though she could take them both out with a single hand.

The innocent man waved her away with the disdain of swatting away an irritating bug. "Just get the whack-job away from me."

She stared into space. Part dazed. Part drained. How had she let this happen? Again? What kind of a cruel joke was it that the universe kept playing on her?

"You're sure, sir?" said Pudgy Guard. "Because we'll have the whole incident on CCTV."

"I appreciate the help," he said, "but please, just get her out of my sight."

The two guards hauled Tess back through the store. A mother pulled her young daughter to her as Tess was bustled past. Shoppers stared. Staff gossiped.

The guards dragged Tess right out through the doors and onto the street. Finally, they released her.

Without being supported by the guards, she staggered, but caught herself.

As if half asleep, she said, "Sorry. I didn't mean to cause any trouble."

"Yeah, well just see you don't come back anytime soon, because the next time, I'll make damn sure that the store presses charges even if the customer won't."

Her legs wobbled and almost gave way. Tess grabbed a lamppost for support. Mentally and physically spent, she slumped against it.

Pudgy Guard sneered and shook his head. "Get a grip, lady. And get yourself clean."

The guards went back into the store but hovered inside the entrance watching her, ensuring she didn't try to enter again.

Tess hung her head and rubbed her brow.

How many times was her mind going to play this cruel trick on her? How many times was she going to see that killer, only for it not to be him? Seventeen years ago, he'd ruined her life; seventeen years later, he was still ruining it.

But she couldn't relive this. Not again. Not now. She had to focus. Had to concentrate on the job she and Bomb were now working on. Distractions could kill just as surely as a bullet in the head. If she let ghosts from her past cloud her mind, the killer she was hunting today would see her long before she saw him. And that could only end one way.

She drew a series of long, slow breaths to help clear her mind and reenergize her body, then tottered away from the lamppost.

Her legs still unsteady, she stumbled back the way she'd come.

Focus. She had to focus.

But how?

The city blurred. She passed people, buildings, vehicles, but she might as well have been alone in a desert for all the sensory information she absorbed.

Finding herself back in Bryant Park, Tess all but collapsed onto one of the green metal chairs scattered along the tree-lined promenade. The chair rocked and almost toppled over, but Tess flung her arms out and spread her feet to keep from crunching into the ground.

Once steady, she leaned back and closed her eyes. Breathed long and slow. Let the fresh air, stillness, and saxophone music transport her to a world of calmness and stability.

Tess shut out everything but the music, the wind gusting through the trees, and her breathing.

Bit by bit, she banished all the chaos that had created such confusion inside her head. Blanked it all out as if her mind was a brand-new canvas. Once her mind was clear, she started filling it with thoughts again, painting ideas on it once more.

Her thinking still unsure, she forced herself to look at the cold hard logic of what she had to do to find Amelia's killer. Logic would ground her. Logic would save her.

But where to start?

Becks. Becks was the key.

Get to Becks. Get the facts. Get the killer.

Simple. Just as logic should be.

Her mind steady once more, her thoughts started to flow more fluidly.

She tensed her leg muscles and readied to push herself up, but sank back onto her seat. She rested her hands on her thighs and gasped another couple of breaths, then tried again. Finally, as if a 200-pound man was pushing on her shoulders to pin her down, Tess heaved herself up off the chair.

She trudged back toward the subway on 6th Avenue. After she'd talked with Becks, she'd go to see Nat. She still needed to know why he'd had an altercation with Amelia, not to mention why he'd felt the need to hide it.

But that was only a minor point. More importantly, as head of the neighborhood watch, Nat might know if TG had been spotted loitering in the area.

She started down into the subway again.

Even after seventeen years… She could've sworn that was him.

"Goddamnit." Tess hammered the side of her fist into the tiled subway wall. Seventeen years and still he was haunting her. Seventeen goddamn years. When would she ever find peace? When would she...

Clawing its way through her questions, a thought dragged her back to the moment.

Tess quickened her pace down the steps.

Nat's 9:00 p.m. neighborhood watch patrols involved him staring into the shadows. Had he seen someone lurking there? And, more crucially, had that someone seen him?

Maybe Nat had been threatened with violence if he said anything.

That meant Becks wasn't the only one who needed protecting.

But who was in the greatest danger?

Who should Tess run to protect first?

Chapter 19

WHETHER IT WAS the stress of Amelia's death, or that she simply needed to tell someone – anyone – what she knew, once Becks sat down opposite Tess in the café, she spewed forth the whole sordid saga of the dangerous double life Amelia had reveled in leading.

"Why haven't you spoken with the police?" asked Tess.

Nursing a coffee at the green table at which Tess had eaten earlier, Becks didn't look up. "I ain't got nothing to tell 'em."

Becks swirled a drop of coffee around and around in the bottom of the cup as if finding the circling liquid soothing, and then said, "I ain't got no proof. I ain't got no lawyer. Last time I tried to help with an investigation, I was the one that got busted."

She looked up from her cup. Her eyes red and swollen, she stared deeply into Tess's eyes as if she believed if she looked deep enough she'd find answers. "Why are all guys worth shit?"

If she expected Tess to give her that answer, hell was she going to be disappointed.

Tess tapped her phone on the table between them. It displayed a photo from Becks's Facebook gallery that Tess had downloaded at the library: Becks, Amelia, and a man all squashed up together to squeeze into a photo taken at arm's length. Each of them grinning, they looked like the best of friends.

Tess said, "And this is him? This is TG?"

Becks said one word. It wasn't *yes* but it couldn't have been a more positive identification. "Bastard."

"But you have no idea where he lives because it was always in public?"

"Up an alleyway, in a bathroom stall, behind a dumpster… It was like if it wasn't in public, he couldn't get off on it. You know?"

"But if he showed no interest in Amelia other than for sex, why did she continue seeing him?"

"Said she loved him. You know? Said he loved her and was gonna take her away from here." Becks shook her head. "Hell, asshole wouldn't even give her his real name so how's he gonna give her a new life?"

"And you told her that?"

"Only every time he showed up. But would she listen?" She swirled the coffee around the cup again. "After one time with his friend Jimmy, I said, 'Girl, that there guy's gonna be the death of you' and even though she knew she done wrong, she still went back for more."

"Jimmy? That was the friend TG persuaded her to have sex with while he watched?"

109

Becks looked up again, tears in her eyes. "Is that love? 'Cause it sure as hell don't sound like love to me."

So when dangerous sex – sex in public places – lost its novelty, TG upped the stakes. Tess sighed. With violence at home and abuse in public, in what kind of hell had Amelia been trapped?

"Was he ever violent towards her?" asked Tess.

"Hell if I know. After I ragged on her over the Jimmy thing, she stopped telling me a lot of stuff." She looked up. "But one time, I seen him with a knife."

"And she was with him last night?"

Becks hung her head. Nodded. Sobbed.

The man in the photo, who they'd christened TG because, as part of his game, he'd refused to give his name, had regularly met Amelia. Wanting a better life than the violent one she shared with Ethan, Amelia had seen TG as her escape route, so she'd pandered to his craving for exhibitionist sex. Sadly, she was merely being used by a sexual predator.

Tess eased a thumb and forefinger into the secret pocket inside the waistband of her trousers, a pocket similar to the one she sewed into all her clothes. Inside, she kept an emergency stash of cash: one thousand dollars. In her line of work, she never knew when she might have to go to ground and get rid of her bank cards to avoid being traced, or be trapped and need to buy her way out of trouble.

It was emergency money.

Strictly emergency.

She'd do absolutely anything to avoid tapping into it.

But emergencies came in many guises.

Tess slid three hundred dollars across the table.

With a deep frown, Becks looked up at her, cheeks streaming with tears.

"Take it," Tess said, "Keep out of sight for a few days. Go see your mom or get a room in Queens. Anything. Just get away from here. You'll be safe and I promise you, when you come back, all this will be over and the person responsible won't hurt anyone ever again." She stood.

Becks peered up through eyes so red, so teary. "Really?"

Tess rested a hand on her shoulder. "I never break my word."

If Ethan hadn't intended on killing TG when he'd gone on the run that morning, he would surely be intent on it now if he'd learned the truth of how this man had so abused *his* woman.

As for TG? Was sexual abuse the worst aspect of Amelia's relationship with him? Or could someone who craved ever greater and greater thrills see murder as the ultimate high?

Chapter 20

ON THE STONE stoop to Nat's apartment building, Tess paused. In what way was Nat involved? She hoped she was about to find a perfectly reasonable explanation for Nat to have had an altercation with Amelia in the dead of night. But... Though other suspects had loomed to the fore, with far stronger motives for violence, sometimes it was the most placid of folk who perpetrated the most horrendous of acts.

Had Nat's similarities to her grandpa clouded her judgment? Could there be a dark side to his sweet nature? Or was he really just a little old man who'd been threatened so needed protection?

She drew a deep breath. She needed answers.

Having to be buzzed in, Tess looked at the names associated with each apartment. All of those listed under the buzzers were scrawled on scraps of whatever paper must first have come to hand. All except one. 'Nathan Ridley' was typed on a piece of crisp, white paper which fitted its slot perfectly.

Her thumb hovered over the buzzer. She hoped she'd find the quiet little man, living the quiet little life, that she'd met just that morning, and not a man with a dark secret he'd do anything to hide.

She pushed the buzzer.

A few seconds later, Nat's voice came through the little speaker. "Yes?"

"Nat? It's Tess Williams. I'm sorry to disturb you again."

"It's a little late, dear."

She glanced at her watch: 7:54 p.m. "I'm sorry, but I need to ask you something, please."

He let her in and immediately busied himself in the kitchen.

"Would you like some tea, dear?"

"No, thank you."

"Coffee?"

She shook her head. "No, thanks."

"Juice?"

"Thanks, but no."

"Oh, I know. I've got some lovely organic carrot cake. Absolutely beautiful with a glass a milk." He smiled at her, eyebrows raised with expectation.

"Nat, really, I'm fine."

She couldn't help but smirk to herself. Her grandpa had been just like that – gracious to the point of irritating. Not just with her, though, but with everyone, because he loved people and loved playing host.

Well…

Maybe she'd received special treatment occasionally.

Okay, often.

Truth be told, nothing was ever too much trouble for her grandpa's little princess. She still occasionally felt pangs of guilt remembering the times she'd played on that. But then, she'd only been a kid. Wasn't that what kids were supposed to do?

But it wasn't the 'special treatment' she missed.

No, it was... the sense of belonging.

Yes, that was it. It was being able to close the door on all the coldness in the world and relax in a home where love lived.

She watched Nat hemming and hawing to himself over whether to put coconut or chocolate chip cookies on a white porcelain plate. She smiled again. Her grandpa hadn't been quite the ditherer that Nat was, but the similarity was uncanny. Bathed in a warm glow, she watched him arrange three coconut cookies on the plate.

Finally, Nat hobbled over to the couch. He walked so slowly his gait was almost in time to the ticking of his deathly slow clock on the mantel.

Sitting beside her, he said, "So, what is it that's so important? Have we caught someone?" He nibbled a cookie.

"Have you seen this man around the neighborhood?" Tess showed him the close-up photo of Becks, Amelia, and TG.

"Oh, there's Amelia, bless her. And her friend Rebecca. Oh, such a lovely photo."

114

"Yes, but have you seen the man?"

"Hmmm..." Nat scrunched up his face, scrutinizing the photo. "Well... I'd like to say yes, but..." He rubbed his chin. "No, I couldn't swear to that." He looked up at her. "Why? Is that who did it?"

"Let's just say he's someone I'd like to talk to."

He pulled her phone closer. "Let me have a better look, dear."

She let him lift her hand right up to his face.

There was more chin rubbing and muttering.

And the clock ticked on. Unbearably loudly in the mausoleum of a room. And the ticking got slower and slower and slower as she waited, and waited, and waited for Nat to reply. It really felt like waiting for death.

Finally, he said, "You know... I wouldn't be able to say hand on Bible, but..."

Nat stood and wandered over to a wooden rolltop desk. He rummaged inside. Not finding what he was looking for, he pulled open one of the drawers. He took out a manila wallet file and thumbed through the loose paper contents, and then took out one of the letter-size papers.

He nodded. "Yes. Yes, it was last weekend. Not on my patrol, but later when I couldn't sleep – those darn good-for-nothing sleeping pills again – I saw someone lurking around outside Amelia's building. When he saw me, he crossed the street and disappeared down that alleyway." He pointed through one of his living room windows.

"The alley in which Amelia's body was found?"

"That very one, dear. Yes."

She held her camera up toward him. "And it could've been this man?"

"The more I think about it, the more I believe it was."

That was a major breakthrough: TG had not been just someone who used to meet Amelia for no-ties sex, he'd been a stalker. He liked to push boundaries; he liked to control others; and most importantly, he liked danger.

What if he really had wanted to take Amelia away from Ethan?

What if she was having second thoughts after the voyeurism incident?

And what if he'd decided that if he couldn't have her no one could?

"Is there anything else I can help you with?" asked Nat.

There was. But could she bring herself to ask?

Chapter 21

TESS FUMBLED FOR words and looked away so she wouldn't catch Nat's eye. "Er... there, er, might be something you can help with, yes."

"Well, spit it out, then, dear. As my old grandpa used to say, you can't grow turnips without sowing turnip seeds."

Nat was such a kindly old man, she didn't want to put him on the spot. Neither did she want to look foolish to him by asking what would appear to be a truly dumb question. But she needed answers.

Finally, Tess said, "When you saw Amelia, was everything okay? There wasn't any unpleasantness between the two of you?"

"Heavens no. Why?"

"The taxi driver—"

"Oh, you found him. Oh, good. Was it my information?"

"Yes. Thank you. It was very helpful. So, anyway, he said he saw you argue with her on Chiltern Avenue."

"Argue? With Amelia? No, I'm afraid he's taken you a bit of a ride there, dear."

The driver had been in no position to indulge in any dancing with a saucepan of scalding chili broiling his crotch. Why would he lie about that?

Tess said, "He was quite adamant."

"Well… to be fair… Amelia was a little, shall we say, colorful with her language when I saw her. But she was only blowing off steam after her fight with Ethan, dear. It was perfectly understandable." He smiled. "Water off a duck's back."

"But why didn't you say anything about it?"

"Because it was of such little consequence it wasn't worthy of bringing to anyone's attention."

She noted he didn't say 'to your attention', but 'to anyone's attention'.

Tess said, "Have you spoken to the police yet?"

"An officer came by this afternoon."

"And you didn't tell him either?"

He laughed. "Oh, my word, Ms. Williams, you'd make an outstanding prosecuting attorney."

He was right – where was the payoff in grilling Nat over something so insignificant to the bigger picture? She'd already discovered that TG had the motive and means for attacking Amelia, and now Nat had confirmed he had been lurking in the area, probably looking for the opportunity. Though the justice system was broken, as a set of criteria, means, motive and opportunity was one thing it had gotten right.

She smiled at Nat. "I'm sorry. I just need to check everything and that nothing's been left out."

"That's perfectly alright, dear. Now" – he winked – "what about that carrot cake?"

Her phone rang.

"Excuse me." She checked caller ID. "I'm sorry, but I have to take this."

"I'll leave you to it, dear."

He picked up his plate and padded over to the kitchen area.

Tess wandered over to the corner of the room farthest away from Nat.

"Hi, what you got?" She purposefully didn't use a name in such a quiet environment. Especially around such a busybody as Nat.

"Your boy," said Bomb.

"Where?"

"The scene of the crime – or at least one of them – Shades."

"Thanks." She hung up and turned to Nat. "I'm heading off, Nat. Thanks for all your help."

"Oh, it's nothing. I'm only doing what any decent person would do."

"You be careful on your patrols. There're a lot of sickos out there."

"Don't you worry about me, dear. You just catch whoever did such an awful thing to poor Amelia."

"You can be sure I'll give it my best shot."

Walking to the door, she couldn't help but ask one last question. "There's nothing else I need to know, is there? It might seem unimportant to you, but it could be vital."

He gazed away into space for a few seconds.

Finally, he said, "I don't believe so, dear. But I'll be sure to let you know if I think of anything."

She pulled the door open as he was walking over to see her out, "Thanks again, Nat."

"Any time, dear. You know where I am if you need me."

As she walked down the stoop onto the street, she looked back. The drapes pulled aside, Nat again waved to her through the security bars at his window. She smiled and nodded to him.

Once this job was over, she'd pop back and have that carrot cake. Maybe buy Nat a book on the strategy of war as a thank-you present.

She smiled to herself. Every moment she spent with Nat, she couldn't help but feel she was with her grandpa again. And how she'd ached for that feeling for so very long. Ached to spend just a few more minutes, just a few more seconds with him. To feel... To feel as if the world wasn't filled only with pain and hardship and deceit, but filled with... with love and with someone who'd smile just because she was there.

She sighed. Yes, he might be boring, might use fifty words where one would do, and he might have the most horrendous taste in décor, but she'd enjoy visiting him again.

At the junction with Chiltern, she hailed a cab – she didn't have time to waste using public transport.

Ethan had obviously decided to stake out Shades and wait for TG. She had to be there. Between them, Ethan and TG were the only people who knew the truth about what had happened to Amelia.

But Becks had said TG carried a knife. Ethan might be mean and muscular, but against a blade, even the biggest biceps sliced like butter. If Tess got there too late, she might discover nothing but a bloody corpse and even more questions.

This could be her one shot at finding the killer.

Finding him and punishing him.

But could she get there in time?

Chapter 22

HARSH SPOTLIGHTS AND headache-inducing strobe effects creating an ambience only matched by the distorted rumbling of the subwoofers, Shades greeted Tess with all the finesse of a wife finding her husband in bed with her sister – raucous, ugly, yet strangely compelling.

At the bar, she bought a bottle of cider and then scanned the room for Ethan, panning across the assortment of smiling, laughing, lonely, frowning, bored, desperate faces.

No sign.

Tess ambled over to a table opposite the main door, where she took a seat with her back against the wall.

Her gaze flicked around the club. She could see the bar, entrance, emergency exit, and restrooms.

After doing this job for so long, deciding where to sit in a public area was no longer a matter of choice but of an almost Pavlovian response – she needed to be in the position where no one could surprise her from behind and from where she could easily reach the doors to get out, or reach whoever had gotten in.

Leaning back, she cradled her bottle. Now it was just a case of waiting.

She took a swig of cider. Cold, sweet and as golden as the morning sun, it was so refreshing it was like downing a glass of Nature itself. When she was on a job looking to befriend someone for information, she drank domestic beer so she would blended in. That not being necessary in this instance, she could enjoy her drink of choice, a drink she'd come across in Europe and loved ever since. She took another mouthful. How easy it would be to kick back and forget about Amelia, sexual abuse, and homicide.

Tess put her bottle on the table. Unfortunately, this was work, not a night on the town. There had been enough distractions already, now she had to prepare for the encounter she was sure was going to come.

She already had on her body armor. At a tad under a thousand bucks, it was the most stealth bullet- and knife-proof vest on the market, but she couldn't risk removing her jacket. While almost invisible under her shirt to the average Joe, the armor might still be visible to those with an eye for such things. She couldn't risk rumors spreading through the club that she was an undercover cop – nothing would spook Ethan quicker.

She scoured the faces again. Only a few minutes earlier, Bomb had confirmed Ethan was still in there, so where was he? It was a good thing it was still early so it wasn't packed tight and she could see most of the clientele.

With no target in sight, her mind wandered back to Bryant Park, back to the subway, back to him.

She could've sworn that was him. Even after all these years.

Eighteen months ago, on the corner of Broadway and West Forty-Second Street, she'd last seen 'him'. She'd been standing waiting to cross the street and he'd casually cruised past her on a bus hanging a right. She'd chased the bus two blocks as it lurched through traffic till it stopped at lights and she got a clear view of the man sitting four seats down by the window. That hadn't been him either. It never was.

On that occasion, it had been the best part of a week before she'd been able to think of anything else and stop reliving the nightmare he'd thrust her into.

She banged her bottle down on the table.

Focus.

She had to focus.

In her line of work, being distracted was like crossing a busy road with your eyes shut – it wasn't a case of if you'd make it across, it was a case of how quickly you'd be nothing but a bloody mass of splattered flesh.

Forcing her mind to quieten, yet again, she scanned the bar's clientele.

But, yet again, that niggling question clawed its way from the back of her mind – what was she missing?

She couldn't even remember now when she'd first had this feeling. Maybe it was merely the subway incident that had so rattled her it was skewing her thoughts. Was there something she wasn't seeing? Or was it just her mind playing tricks?

A tall man strutted toward her. He flicked his long brown bangs out of his face by throwing his head backwards.

She knew that cocky arrogance. Great. This was all she needed.

Resting his hands on her table, he leaned down to her. "I haven't seen you in here before."

"No." She leaned to her left to try to look around him so she wouldn't miss Ethan.

He leaned to his right to remain in front of her. "Let me buy you a drink and give you three reasons you should sleep with me tonight."

Did lines like that ever work except in male fantasies?

She smiled. "Can we start with a kiss?"

He grinned. "Sure." He leaned in.

"You got a breath mint first? I blew a Syrian taxi driver earlier, and I bet I don't have to tell you how that taste lingers."

He pulled back, face twisted in disgust. "Jesus, what's your problem?" He scurried away to his friends.

For a moment, she closed her eyes.

Forget the subway incident. Forget 'him'. Forget dumb niggling questions.

Focus. Get Ethan. Get answers. Get the job done.

Simple.

Opening her eyes, she took another swig of cider.

Again, she panned face to face to face. Ethan had to be here. Had to be. Unless he'd had his phone stolen, which meant Bomb was tracking the wrong person. Or he'd seen too many cop shows, so wary of someone tracking him through cell towers, he'd dumped it. Either way, she'd be screwed.

But was Ethan either that lucky or that smart?

Briefly removing her backpack, she retrieved her black leather armored gloves.

The custom-made gloves looked innocent enough except under the very closest of scrutiny, yet, secreted within, ergonomically crafted titanium alloy inserts cocooned her hands. Only one-tenth of an inch thick, the inserts were barely discernible through the leather.

She examined them. Surreptitiously, under the table, just to be safe.

Running her fingertips over the metal and the thin inner layer of latex foam rubber which provided a modicum of cushioning inside, she checked for damage to the plate that covered the back of each hand and wrapped around the pinkie side of it before spreading across the palm.

She then felt along the segmented sections that lay over the knuckles and partway down each finger to ensure there were no sharp edges and the segments hinged freely.

All the while, she scanned the bar's drinkers for any sign of her target.

People came, people went, people milled and mixed, chatted and posed. But nowhere was Ethan.

Under the table, Tess continued examining her gloves. Flipping the hinged section across the heel of the palm of the left glove, then the right, she checked for unrestricted movement for her thumbs.

Everything seemed okay.

Tess had broken bricks with her bare hands. But that was in a dojo in Kyoto where the bricks weren't moving, let alone trying to hit her back. Hands were surprisingly delicate. If you misjudged it, a simple punch could break your knuckles or fingers, leaving you one-handed and vulnerable. That was why boxers taped up their hands and wore padded gloves – protection.

But titanium alloy being harder than steel, her gloves didn't only protect her – they gave her hand strikes the stopping power of a hammer.

She slipped on her gloves. The metal inserts cocooned her hands perfectly. She was ready.

But ready for what?

Again, she scanned the bar. Scanned the doorways, scanned all the tables, scanned all the people reveling in the joys of night life.

Nothing.

Absolutely nothing.

Maybe Bomb had been wro—

There!

Across the far side of the bar, Ethan strode toward the men's room.

Chapter 23

NONCHALANTLY, SHE STOOD and followed Ethan.

The prospective confrontation causing her stomach to quake, Tess calmed herself with her four-second breathing technique.

A small man with a cheeky smile stepped in front of her. He grinned. "Can I get you a drink?"

"No, thanks." She sidestepped to her right to move around him.

He moved left to stay in front of her and held up three ten-dollar bills. "I hear you like BJs. Wanna fit me in some time?"

He obviously thought if it was true she was blowing taxi drivers, it was because she was short of cash, and if it wasn't true, it would be a good laugh at her expense.

"Thanks." She snatched the money. "I'll pencil you in for a week from Tuesday."

She barged him out of the way with her shoulder and stormed toward the restroom.

He turned. "Hey!"

Easing the restroom door open, Tess peeked in.

Grappling on the floor, Ethan struggled with another man.

Limbs flailed, smacked, pushed, and clawed.

Bodies gasped, grunted, cursed, and groaned.

Flung onto his back, the other man's face became visible – TG. Why hadn't she seen him? He must have been in here already, or had snuck in while one of those two sleazeballs was trying to romance her.

Tess watched. If they exhausted each other, it would make her job much easier.

Sprawled on the gray slate tiles, Ethan pinned TG in a headlock. TG bit his forearm.

Ethan swore and pulled away.

TG rolled across the floor. Whipped out a switchblade.

They both slowly clambered up, warily watching each other.

Ethan stabbed a finger at TG. "You're gonna bleed, you fuck. I'm gonna stick your knife in your fucking neck."

TG sneered. "The bitch was begging for it. If I hadn't done her someone else would have."

Ethan lunged at him.

TG slashed his knife.

Tess ripped Ethan out of the way by his arm so the blade passed harmlessly by. He tumbled against the sinks and crashed to the floor.

She turned to TG.

TG waved his blade at her. "You want some, bitch?"

She had on her body armor, but if he sliced an artery in her leg or arm, she'd bleed out almost as quickly as if he slit her throat. Blades were a danger that had to be closed down as quickly as possible.

She stared at him. Her voice calm, unwavering, she said, "Try it. If you're man enough."

TG slashed at her.

Tess blocked his knife arm and trapped it close to her body to immobilize it.

She smashed her palm heel into his face.

Tightened the lock on his elbow joint.

Stripped the blade from his loosened grip.

He struggled to pull free.

She kneed him in the thigh to deaden his leg.

Head-butted him in the face.

He cried out. Staggered back. Hands covering his nose.

She kicked him in the gut.

He gasped and reeled into the middle stall. Fell over the toilet. Collapsed in a heap.

Music blared as the restroom door opened.

Tess whirled around, wary of another threat.

The two guys who'd propositioned her stood in the restroom doorway, mouths agape.

Tess pointed. "Get out!"

Scrambling, they fought with each other to get out first.

She saw Ethan clambering to his feet. She grabbed his hand, twisted to lock the wrist, then spun him around. He twirled, almost balletically, into the white porcelain urinals and crashed to the floor.

Whipping two nylon zip ties from her pocket, she grabbed TG. Still holding his knife so no one else could use it against her, she yanked him out of the stall and strapped his left hand to one stall door's handle, then his right to a handle two stalls away. On his knees facing her, he hung, suspended.

Tess turned to Ethan.

Groggy, face down in the urinal trough, he floundered as he tried to push up.

Tess stamped on his lower back.

He sprawled across the floor.

With one knee, she knelt on his back to pin him and yanked his head back by his hair.

She slammed his face against the porcelain. "Tell me what happened last night."

"Get off, you crazy bitch."

"Jesus, if I had a dime for every time someone's called me that." She slammed his head against the urinal again. "You were seen fighting with Amelia. Tell me what happened."

His cheek and mouth squashed against the porcelain, Ethan said, "*He* happened. *He* fucking happened."

She hammered her fist between his shoulder blades.

Ethan groaned and arched back.

With the pain distracting him, Tess slipped a zip tie around his ankles before he even knew it.

She shoved Ethan aside and made for TG.

Music blared again. She looked around. In the doorway stood a black dude in a purple shirt.

She shouted, "Get out."

The dude in the entrance said, "Everything alright, miss?"

She pointed the knife. "I said, 'out'!"

The dude held his hands up defensively as he backed away. "Hey, no worries."

Tess turned back to TG, his face running with blood from a gash on the bridge of his nose.

She pressed the switchblade against his cheek. "How about we see just how sharp this is?"

TG smirked.

Tess leaned closer. "You will tell me what I want to know."

But he snickered and shook his head. He was either really dumb and had a death wish or really brave and had a cunning plan.

The hairs prickled on the back of her neck at the thought that it could be the latter.

Chapter 24

TESS'S FEET FLEW from under her and she crunched into the floor. The knife skidded across the tiles.

TG shouted, "Kill the bitch, Jimmy. Kill her."

A heavy kick smacked into her ribs.

Tess yelped, but fought her instinct to curl into a defensive ball. Doing that, she might just as well stick a sign on her back saying 'please kick me.'

She twisted.

Grabbed Jimmy's foot.

Rammed her shoulder into his shins.

Jimmy crashed to the floor.

She rolled onto his legs.

Hammered her elbow into his crotch. And again. And again.

He squealed so high-pitched it was like a small animal.

He leaned forward to try to protect himself.

She slammed a backfist into his jaw.

His head flew back and smashed into the floor. He lay still.

So that was Jimmy. TG's comrade in voyeurism. Why hadn't she thought of him showing up? Talk about a rookie mistake.

She climbed to her feet. Looked around.

"Goddamn it."

Ethan had disappeared. In his place lay the knife and a cut zip tie.

Now she'd have to contact Bomb. Start the whole hunt over again. Except this time, it would be ten times harder because this time Ethan would know he wasn't paranoid: someone really was after him.

She scowled at TG.

He pulled back into the middle stall as far as his binds would allow, the nylon cutting into his wrists. "Please. I'm sorry. I don't want trouble."

She prowled over to him. "Too late. Trouble's here." She pounded her steel-clad fist into his gut.

He wheezed and doubled over.

She bound Jimmy's hands with another zip tie and then checked his wallet. James Iverson had fifty-six dollars and change. She left the coins.

TG tried to pull back into the stall when she turned to him. "My wallet's in my back pocket. Take it. Please. Take everything."

"Thank you." She did. Henderson 'TG' Sumpter donated ninety-two dollars towards making the world a better place.

Henderson smiled feebly, probably believing that his money had placated her.

How wrong could someone be?

She grabbed him by the throat, her fingers clawed around his windpipe. He made strange gargling sounds.

Tess stared deep into his eyes, eyes that were screwed up with pain. "Why did you kill Amelia Ortega?"

His eyes opened. Opened wide.

She relaxed her grip.

He spluttered, then spoke, his voice rasping. "What...? Amelia... Amelia's dead?" He struggled to swallow.

His eyes widened again as his mind worked out why this was happening to him. "And you think I had something to do with it?"

She released her grip on him. Strolled away. Under such circumstances, you couldn't fake a reaction like that: he wasn't the killer.

She ripped open the restroom door, but stopped.

A simple beating wasn't enough. Even if it had been by a woman.

She paced back.

Henderson's voice rasped still. "Please, please. I didn't do it. I didn't even know."

"This is for humiliating a woman." She hammered her steel fist into his groin.

He gasped with barely a sound, his eyes so wide Tess thought his eyeballs might fall out of his head.

"This..."

She slammed a fist into his face. His head flew back. Blood and broken teeth fell to the tiled floor.

"… is in case you're ever tempted to try it again." With a crooked nose and missing teeth, he'd find it much harder to manipulate women.

Reaching around his waist, she unfastened Henderson's trousers with little effort, him groggy from her headshot.

"And this…" She pulled them down only to find tighty whities. "Really? Your mom buy you those?"

She shook her head, hoping that once she'd removed his underwear there'd be something inside that would've made it worthwhile for a woman in a long-term relationship to risk losing everything. There wasn't.

Him now half-naked, she said, "This is for every woman you've ever lied to just to get laid."

How much would he like humiliation games and exhibitionism when he was the one abused? Especially when it would be all over YouTube within minutes for everyone he knew to laugh at.

Tess leaned right down to his ear. "If you don't want us to meet again, learn to respect women."

She took a quick photo of each of their driver's licenses on her phone, chucked the licenses in the urinal trough, and then stalked out.

Okay, things hadn't quite gone to plan, but even though she hadn't caught the killer, at least she'd identified him – Ethan. Now, how the hell was she going to find him again?

Chapter 25

DESPITE KNOWING IT was pointless, she searched the faces in the crowded bar for Ethan's as she dashed for the exit.

God, the world was twisted. Well, no, the world was just fine – it was the goddamn people who infested it that were twisted. This job was all about obsession. Twisted obsession. In a jealous rage, Ethan had killed Amelia and now he'd tried to kill the man who'd dared to lay hands on his prize possession.

Choices. How easily people let emotion cloud their judgments. And how easily misjudgments ruined lives.

Amelia had chosen infidelity in the hope of bringing joy into her miserable life.

Ethan had chosen violence as a way to control a disintegrating relationship.

TG had chosen exploitation to gain what he believed would make him happy.

Choices. People chose their own paths so only had themselves to blame for the hell to which those paths led. How easy it would have been for Ethan, Amelia, or TG to have made a different choice so this dire situation would never have arisen.

Outside Shades, Tess glanced up and down the street.

Ethan was nowhere in sight. She scoured the faces of the pedestrians enjoying their night on the town. Where the devil was he?

She grabbed her phone for Bomb to get a new location on Ethan, but stopped. "Oh, hell." What was it she'd said to Ethan: 'You were seen fighting with Amelia.'?

She stamped her foot in frustration "Shit!" God, she could be so stupid.

Nat had witnessed the fight. Past 2:00 a.m., he was likely the only one to have done so. What if Ethan figured that out? Especially if he feared being arrested and facing a trial?

It was obvious what he'd do. She might as well have painted a target on Nat's back.

Worse still, Ethan had a head start on her.

Whipping her head first to her left, then to her right, she scoured the street for a taxi.

Nothing.

"Come on. Come on."

She stepped off the curb for a better view around a number of parked vehicles.

Nothing.

"Oh, for Christ's sake."

Could she get there in time to catch Ethan?

Could she get there in time to save Nat?

Chapter 26

"YES, I KNOW how late it is, but..." In the back of the yellow cab, Tess held the phone away from her ear. Nat wouldn't stop babbling about how late it was and how discourteous a phone call was at such an ungodly hour, even from a friend.

She rolled her eyes and muttered, "For the love of God."

Putting the phone back to her ear, she tried again. "Nat..."

Still talking.

"Nat..."

Still talking.

She raised her voice, "Nat!"

He stopped.

She said, "Please, just listen to me: don't open your door to anyone until I get there. Promise me."

She shook her head and rubbed her brow. She wanted to strangle him herself.

"Yes, I know I'm being very dramatic," said Tess, "but just do it, please. Okay?"

The taxi driver glanced back. "Everything alright, lady?"

Some guys could pull off the unshaven look. Rugged handsomeness oozing from every pore. Others just looked like they lived on a park bench. Unfortunately for him, the driver lay firmly in the latter category.

With a wave of her hand, she gestured everything was fine.

Still on the phone, she said, "Okay, thank you, Nat... Yes... Yes, I'll be there just as quickly as I can." She hung up.

She groaned with frustration. God, it was like trying to get through to an awkward child. She wouldn't mind, but she was sure he wasn't really that old. He was likely one of those guys who'd already appeared middle-aged when he'd barely graduated college.

But thank God he had security bars at his windows. On the first floor, he'd have been a sitting duck without those. And it would make her job easier – there'd be only one point of entry Ethan could exploit.

Scrolling through her phone's address book, she called Detective Pete McElroy.

A man answered. "Detective McElroy's phone, Detective Harding speaking."

"Can I speak to Mac, please?"

"I'm sorry, he's just stepped out for a moment. I'm his partner. Can I help, ma'am?"

Tess took a slow breath. Did she really want to get involved with yet another cop?

"Ma'am? Are you still there?"

No, she didn't want to get involved. But if she wanted access to privileged information to be able to do her job, she had no choice.

She said, "Hello, Detective Harding. This is Tess Williams. We met at the crime scene this morning."

"Oh, the comedienne, yeah. What can I do for you, Ms. Williams?"

"I've got information on two suspects whose DNA you'll want to eliminate from the Amelia Ortega case."

"Er… okay." He sounded thrown. "We do have a number of unidentified samples, yes. Do you have their names? A description?"

"Henderson Sumpter and James Iverson. I'll send their photos to Mac's phone."

"Great. Thanks. And can I ask how you came by this information?"

"Sure." She hung up. He could ask whatever he wanted. Didn't mean he'd get an answer.

Apart from banging a number of detectives to obtain privileged information, it helped if she threw them a bone every so often. This Josh Harding might be useful at some time in the future – now that he knew she could provide quality information, he'd be more forthcoming if that time ever came.

She glanced at her watch. Every second that ticked by was one second more Ethan had to reach Nat before she did and torture him for ratting him out.

She leaned forward. "Can we go any faster, please? This is an emergency."

"Lady," said the driver, "I don't know what drama you got going, but I got a wife and kids. I ain't getting pulled over."

Pulled over 'for nothing' was what he really meant. Money had a way of swaying the judgment of even the most steadfast of people.

Holding up banknotes, she leaned right up to the plexiglass divider that protected the driver from aggressive passengers. "There's an extra fifty if you put your foot down."

The driver snorted a laugh. "This ain't no movie, lady. I ain't putting my foot nowhere for fifty bucks."

Protecting his livelihood was fair enough. After all, not all drivers were as desperate as Amir. But she had to reach Nat. Had to reach him before Ethan did.

This was no time to quibble about money.

She pulled off her right armored glove and reached into the secret pocket inside her waistband. She whipped out the remaining bills from her emergency stash and shoved them through a gap in the plexiglass divider so they fell beside the driver.

She said, "Seven hundred bucks. You going to put your foot down now, or do I have to put my foot somewhere?"

The driver said nothing. But a burst of speed threw her back into her seat.

Tess gazed at the buildings flying by. She had to reach Nat. Had to. Usually, she was little more than a clean-up crew – arriving after a crime, her only option was to punish those who'd hurt an innocent victim. It was rare she got the opportunity to actually intervene; to not merely take a life, but to grant one and make a real, tangible difference. Such occasions were precious.

Of course, punishing the guilty was rewarding. But knowing you'd given someone a life they wouldn't otherwise have had… Well, that was how a surgeon must feel cutting out a tumor that everyone else believed to be inoperable – unbelievably gratifying.

Plus, this particular life wasn't just any old life. This was Nat's. This was a life that had touched her more than most. This one, she was determined to save. This one, she was going to save.

But the buildings and the pedestrians on the sidewalk stopped speeding by.

She frowned through the passenger window.

The taxi was slowing down.

She looked ahead.

"Oh, for God's sake."

Red stop lights reared out of the darkness.

She rubbed her brow as the taxi slowed to a crawl.

Leaning forward again, she said, "Can we go a different way?"

"You want a rental to drive yourself, lady, feel free."

With such a pleasant demeanor, she wondered how often the driver received tips. But he was right – he knew the city streets far better than she did.

Snorting with resignation, she leaned back.

This was taking too long. Ethan's head start wasn't big, but it was big enough for a burly young guy to cripple a little old one.

No matter how she tried, she couldn't stop her mind conjuring horrific images of what Ethan might be doing to Nat that very second. She struggled not to think of Nat's blood on that hideous brown-and-gold carpet of his. Struggled not to think of his heart slowing to a dead stop just as was her taxi.

Trying to clear her thoughts of an old battered body laying at an unnatural angle on an old battered carpet, she pulled off her other glove to inspect them both. She ran her fingers inside them to check for damage. Even though she knew there was none.

But still the images of blood and pain and a lifeless body haunted her.

She glanced up. Ahead, the light was still red. Like some sick joke.

She glared at the light.

It mocked her.

"Come on."

One blazing red eye gazed back at her, as if it had all the time in the world.

"Oh, for the love of God."

The light all but laughed at her predicament.

And suddenly…

Green.

The people and streets once more flew by.

She gazed ahead through the windshield.

How much farther was it?

The taxi sped on.

It swung out wide and passed a bus. Cut back in front of a red SUV.

The SUV blared its horn.

But the taxi was already swerving around a black sedan.

The taxi hammered down the street.

Weaving in and out, in and out.

It screeched around a hard left turn. Flung Tess against her door.

She pushed herself upright. Peered at the buildings.

Where were they? How close were they?

She had to get there. Had to save Nat.

On her right, the subway station she'd exited that morning to reach the crime scene shot by.

Oh, thank God. She was close now. So very close. But was she close enough? Had she been quick enough?

Under her breath, she said, "Come on."

Her gloves fine, she pulled them back on. Balled both fists.

She was ready.

Moments later the taxi pulled up to the curb. Finally!

Tess leapt out.

She shot down the street.

Her guards bounced in her backpack. She'd have to strap them on in Nat's bathroom. Even though she'd always intended on leaving the taxi a block away to hide her destination from the taxi driver, she couldn't have risked putting them on in the car and having him witness her preparations in case something went wrong later and the police traced him.

In the distance, the glowing red neon sign for A Taste of Napoli taunted her about how far away she was still.

She sprinted toward it.

Nearing the corner to Nat's street, her heart hammered. Not with the exertion of running, but with what might be lying in wait: police cruisers, crime scene tape, the coroner's truck…

She prayed she wasn't too late.

Rounding the corner, she found nothing but a quiet, dimly lit street. Not that such a sight stopped her heart from thumping.

Nat's building reared before her, black and foreboding. Other than the checkered pattern of lit windows, nothing suggested anyone stirred inside. Anything could be happening in there. Anything. Right now.

Arms pumping, heart pounding, Tess raced along the sidewalk.

What would she find at Nat's?

A smiling old man and carrot cake?

Or a bloody corpse and endless self-recrimination?

Chapter 27

"SO YOU HAVEN'T seen or heard anyone?" Tess peered through the barred window into the lurking darkness outside. In the background, Nat's clock ticked as slowly and as ominously as ever.

"No, dear. No one."

As usual, Nat stood at his kitchen counter fussing with drinks and baked goods as if the Queen of England had dropped in for a spot of afternoon tea. Still, if it kept him busy it would distract him from the impending threat.

Considering the predicament he was in, he was surprisingly calm. The resilience of old folks always amazed her. People always thought of retirees as helpless, infirm buffoons who needed mollycoddling like children, but often in times of crisis, old folks stepped up and really surprised you.

Nat limped over and set a tray of tea and carrot cake down on his table.

"Come. Sit down, dear. You look exhausted."

There was little point in doing anything else right now so she joined him.

Sitting down to tea and cake on the couch, she pulled off her armored leather gloves and stuffed them into her backpack. She still had on her stealth body armor, but hadn't yet donned her shin and forearm guards – as Ethan hadn't broken in before she'd arrived, it looked like he was biding his time until there were as few potential witnesses awake as possible. He likely wouldn't show before midnight. Maybe he was smarter than she'd thought.

Nat said, "I brewed a full teapot, dear. If you've been on the go all day, you're probably dehydrated."

He was right: to remain mentally alert, with muscles supple and ready for action, she made a point of drinking at every opportunity. She picked up the tea and drank.

She said, "Earl Grey. Hmmm." There was nothing as refreshing as a good quality tea.

"At my age, what am I saving up for?"

So buying quality tea was Nat's idea of high living? She smiled.

It always puzzled her why tea wasn't more popular in the USA. She couldn't live without it. But that was likely because she'd spent so long in the Far East, where tea could be not merely a drink but an occasion. She'd loved tea ever since. Except first thing in the morning: she loved a strong coffee as a mental and biological kick start.

"Tell me, dear, why do you believe Ethan will come looking for me?"

"I'm almost sure he's responsible for Amelia's death. And you're the eyewitness who saw them fighting in the street."

The clock ticked on. It seemed even louder than before.

He slid a plate across the table to her with six slices of carrot cake arranged in a fan.

"Almost sure? Why only 'almost'? Don't you have enough evidence?"

She placed a piece of cake on a little porcelain plate, beside the delicate pink flower painted just off-center.

"The police have a number of DNA samples from the scene. Hopefully, they'll nail Ethan by matching his to a sample taken from one of Amelia's wounds." She bit into the cake. "Hmmm, this *is* nice."

"So why can't we just call the police and tell them to arrest Ethan, dear? Isn't that what they're there for?"

These days, the police department was just as susceptible to economic instability as every other business and organization. Not to mention incompetence, corruption, and disinterest. What good cops there were didn't have the time to babysit every single witness to every single crime for fear that the suspect just *might* show up to silence them. Understaffed, underfunded, and crippled by bureaucracy, it was amazing they solved the number of crimes they did.

"They're doing their best," said Tess, "but they're spread pretty thin a lot of the time."

Considering a brutal killer could be lurking outside his door that very second, Nat was remarkably unflustered. She watched him pour her more tea. His hand was steady. Breathing calm.

He said, "So if *you* don't catch Ethan, he might never be caught?"

"I don't want to paint things as bad as that, but…" Tess shrugged.

"So you're Amelia's best hope for justice."

"Well…" She drank her tea to wash down the cake. "You have to try, don't you? It's like you trying to make the world a safer place with your neighborhood watch – every tiny bit helps, doesn't it?"

"It does, dear. But for me, come nine twenty at night, after my patrol, I'm safely here at home and can get on with my life. But I get the impression you see this more as a calling. Something you have to see through to the bitter end, no matter what?"

"If I can stop a crime, or catch the person responsible for one, but choose not to, doesn't that make me just as bad as the criminals themselves?"

The clock ticked. Ticked as if it were waiting for someone. Or something.

"So you won't stop until you catch Ethan?"

"One way or the other, he's going to pay for what he did to Amelia."

"And what if he didn't do it?"

"Then I'll find whoever did." She ate the last mouthful of her cake.

He gestured to the plate on the table. "More cake?"

150

"You're right – it's lovely, but no. Thank you."

If Ethan hadn't done it, she was back to square one: no clues, no suspects, no options. If he was innocent, there was a chance forensic analysis could turn up something else. But that relied on databases like IAFIS and CODIS, so if a person's fingerprints or DNA weren't on file, they couldn't be identified no matter how much evidence the police had.

She stared down at the little pink flower on the white porcelain plate in her lap. Such a delicate flower. Such a delicate plate.

But who else could the killer be? If not Ethan, TG, or Amir, who? It was way too brutal to be a senseless killing. An opportunistic killer wouldn't go to all that trouble of impaling a body for no reason. And who carries a rock hammer just on the off chance they'll find someone to beat with it? No, Amelia hadn't just been murdered, she'd been punished. It was not an opportunistic killing.

So was it a psychopath? Someone deranged? Someone just starting out on a crusade and this would be the first of his many victims?

But why smash in Amelia's face? It was almost as if he wanted to silence her. Even in death. That suggested he knew her. You only silenced those who knew you and who knew something about you that you didn't want others to discover.

Nat stood and picked up the empty plates on which they'd had cake.

Tick… Tick… Tick…

"Nat?"

"Yes, dear?"

She watched him hobble over to the kitchen area to wash his dishes. The only thing standing between Nat and a brutal killer who impaled his victims was a young woman he'd known less than a day. Yet here they were enjoying tea and cake. Why was he so calm? Why wasn't he frightened? It was almost as if he believed there was no danger. He was an intelligent man so why would he think that?

Tess said, "Are you sure you didn't see anyone else around last night?"

"Not that I remember. Why?"

She looked at him standing at the counter. Looked at his bad leg.

"If I catch Ethan, but he turns out to be innocent, that means the killer's still out there. And we have no idea who it is."

He hobbled to one of the cupboards. "I suppose so, dear. But that's hardly likely, is it?"

She watched him, how his body was like hinged wood, not supple and elegant the way a body should be, but awkward and restricted. Her gaze glided over to his cane, standing propped against the side of the couch.

Tick… Tick… Tick… Tick… Tick—

"What time did you say you got home from the store after fighting with Amelia?"

Nat laughed. "Oh, you could hardly call it fighting, dear."

Tess studied Nat's cane. His black wooden cane with a large polished chrome handle. A T-shaped handle. A handle shaped kind of like a rock hammer.

"No?" she said. "So what would you call it?"

Hands on the edge of the sink, he hung his head.

"I knew you were never going to stop. Just knew it." He shook his head. "I gave you Ethan as a suspect, the taxi driver, that man from the photo you showed me – why couldn't you just pick one of them? Or pick none of them and decide the case couldn't be solved? Why couldn't you just…" He threw one of his china cups into the sink. It shattered, bits flying out. "… just let it go?"

"What are you saying, Nat?"

"What am I saying?" He sniggered. He looked around at her. "Do you know how long I've lived here? Sixty-six years. That's how long. Sixty-six wonderful years. And that vicious little bitch was going to take it all away from me."

"Oh God, no."

"She left me no choice, did she? I wasn't going to lose everything because some cheap slut spread gossip about me. A pedophile. *Me!* She said she was going to put my photo on Facebook. Said she was going to spread her lies all over the Internet."

"So you killed her?"

He slumped against the counter. "It was an accident."

"An accident!? Nat, you impaled her on a goddamn pole."

153

"I only meant to smash her phone with my cane. But she turned, didn't she? Got it full in the throat and stopped breathing. So I had to do something. And what better way to make the police believe it was a jealous lover, or a whacko rapist, or a serial killer? Anything but an ordinary person. Anything but me."

She looked at Nat. Feeble old Nat.

He was Sixty-six years old – ancient to Tess, but hardly decrepit in reality. Amelia was such a tiny thing, if she'd weighed 110 pounds it would only have been after a heavy meal. Still, could he have lifted her?

Rage could give a person extraordinary strength, strength to overcome all manner of threatening circumstances. But such strength came at a hefty cost. In moments of extreme stress, the brain reacted by releasing adrenaline to boost strength and endurance. Unfortunately, a side effect was this reaction sapped the mind of balanced thought, transforming a rational person into a primal creature of dark needs and savage actions. It was no mistake that a state of rage was also called 'blind fury.'

"Oh God, Nat... Look, maybe we can claim extenuating circumstances."

Tess stood, but fell back to the couch, her legs wobbling and unable to support her. What the hell...?

"We? Since when is it we? Will you be in the next cell?"

Her head felt thick, like soup you could stand a fork in. The room started to spin. She shook her head to try to clear it, but that just made her feel woozy. She laid her head back on the couch, blinking her eyes to try to focus on the ceiling.

Nat appeared beside her. "I didn't mean to hurt her. Really, I didn't. Only to smash her phone. But someone like me can't go to prison. I wouldn't last a week."

Tess tried to push up but barely had the strength to talk.

"Nat... what... what have you done?"

Chapter 28

A WOMAN SCREAMED.

Lights flickered in front of Tess. She heaved her heavy, heavy eyelids half open, but they fell shut again. She struggled again. Gradually, they fluttered open. The world slowly sharpened into focus.

Nat hovered around his reenactment model muttering to himself. On the table in front of the couch lay an odd selection of objects, amongst them a meat cleaver, an ice pick, a bottle of pills, a glass of milky fluid, a leather belt, pajama bottoms cord, a foot-long screwdriver, and a hammer.

On the TV in the corner, a shadowy figure crept up behind a teenage girl and ran his knife into her back. She screamed. So loudly. And blood splattered everywhere.

Despite the movie, Tess could still hear that damn clock. Each tick pounded in her head like a mallet. She tried to raise her hand, but it caught on something. She looked down. Seated on a wooden dining chair, she'd been tied around the elbows to the back uprights with what looked like her own nylon zip ties, while her legs were bound to the chair legs.

"Nat..." She managed no more than a whisper. "Nat." Louder.

At his window, he stopped muttering and looked over. "You just couldn't let it go, could you? Just couldn't let it go. All you had to do was walk away and say the case was unsolvable. You said yourself the police are stretched – why did you have to decide this case had to be one of those they solved?"

Tied at the elbows, Tess could still move her forearms. But not enough to escape. She tested her binds. Talk about stupid – she wouldn't have bought the ties if they were easily snapped.

Her legs were equally well secured. Tied at the knee, she could probably stand, but she wouldn't be able to run or fight. She needed time.

Tess looked across at him. "Stop, Nat. Please. Before it's too late."

"It's already too late. Do you think a man like me would survive prison?" He shook his head. "I'm a good person. I don't deserve this."

"So if you're a good person, let me go."

"Because you promise you won't tell the police? Promise they won't come and rifle through all my private things. Won't take fingerprints and DNA? Won't ruin me, innocent or not?" He shook his head again.

His 'private things'? 'Fingerprints and DNA'? Everyone had a past. Was there something in Nat's he was eager to keep buried?

157

That made him all the more dangerous.

Her only hope was to not play the victim, but to play the woman who'd befriended him – humanize herself so she wasn't merely an object he could dispose of, but a living, breathing person, just like him.

"Nat, think what you're doing. A good person wouldn't do this. I've got a life. People who love me. Dreams I—"

Marching over, he shouted. "Shut up! Just shut up and let me think."

He looked at the objects on the table. He must have collected everything in his home that he figured would make a decent implement with which to kill her. He picked up the ice pick, but put it down immediately. He weighed the hammer in his hand and took a practice swing, but put that down too. How long had she been out? How many times had he practiced the death blow? And more to the point, why wasn't she already dead?

For an ordinary person, it wasn't easy to take a life. Especially up close. It was one thing to pull a trigger from a distance, but within arm's length? You could see into your victim's eyes, see their hopes and dreams dying right before you when they realized there was no escape. Killing so coldly was a mighty big thing.

A hammer, a knife, a rope…?

In a blind fury, or in a life-or-death struggle, yes, a person could kill with such weapons. But beating, stabbing, or strangling someone to death while they were bound in a chair? That took a tremendous strength of will which few people could muster. Few normal people.

"Please, Nat… think about what you're doing."

He stood for a moment and took a deep breath, eyes closed.

"Nat. Talk to me. Please."

When he opened his eyes again, his voice had that usual calmness and innocence. "You want to talk? Okay, let's talk. But don't think of screaming. Upstairs is vacant" – he pointed to his right – "and there's a storage room. And anyone walking by in the hall will hear that." He pointed to the slasher movie.

Smart thinking. In fact, it was a technique she'd used herself. But then his hobby was studying the strategy of war; he obviously had a very logical mind. He must have. The way he'd played her. Told her about Ethan, about TG being in the area, about the taxi driver. Hell, she couldn't have screwed this one up more if she'd tried. And all because he'd reminded her of her grandpa so she'd had feelings for him. That was where having feelings for someone got you! Hell, talk about dumb.

He pulled another dining chair across and sat before her.

"So…" Unblinking, he locked her with an intense stare. "Let's talk."

Chapter 29

NAT THREW HER armored gloves into her lap. "What are these?"

"I rollerblade. They're protectors for my hands for when I fall."

He nodded. "And these?" He flicked the tie holding her left arm.

"I grow tomatoes in my kitchen. I got these to tie them to stakes."

He nodded again. "Okay."

Without a word, he ripped open her shirt. Buttons scattered across the floor.

While its stealth design allowed her to discreetly wear it under her clothes, it was nonetheless obvious what it was – a bulletproof vest.

"I'm a writer. I told you. I was supposed to be going for a police ride-along tonight."

He leaned closer. Not threatening in any way, but calm. Terrifyingly calm.

He said, "Do you really think I'm so stupid, dear? Who are you? Who knows you're here?"

Tess whimpered. "Okay, okay. Please. Don't hurt me. I'll do anything you say."

"So tell me who knows you're here."

Tess's face screwed up. Her chin quivered. "My editor. My editor knows I'm here."

"You said you were freelance." He held up her cell phone. "Show me your editor's name and number."

Tess's face scrunched up. She sobbed.

"No one knows, do they, dear? You haven't told anyone?"

He stood. Walked over to his arsenal of killing implements. He returned with the glass of milky fluid. He leaned down and held it to her lips.

"Drink this, dear, and it will all be over soon."

Poison: the coward's weapon of choice.

She pulled away. "No. Please."

"It won't hurt. I promise. You won't feel a thing. You'll just drift off to sleep like you did before. But this time... for a little longer."

So that was how he'd knocked her cold earlier – some concoction of his superstrong painkillers and sleeping pills in her tea.

She whimpered again. Slowly shook her head. "Please." Her voice squeaked, the way women's voices go off the scale in times of deep emotional stress. "Please. Don't kill me like this."

He moved the glass to her lips again. "Please, dear. Don't make me fetch the hammer."

Her voice rose even higher in pitch.

161

He leaned closer. "I can't hear you, dear. Say what you need to say and then we'll get it all over with."

She shook her head. "I can't die like this. If I don't confess, I'll go to hell."

"But I'm not a priest, dear."

She squeaked something unintelligible again. Hunched over. Sobbed.

"Okay, okay. Say what you need to say." He leaned down even closer.

She squeaked.

"I can't hear, dear, you'll have to speak up."

She squeaked again.

"What was that?" He leaned even closer.

Too close.

She clamped her teeth right over his nose. Bit. Hard.

He screeched.

She grabbed each of his arms. Pushed up with her legs. Lurched forward.

He fell over backwards and crashed onto his muddy brown carpet. In her chair, Tess landed on top of him, still clamped to his nose and each arm.

He screamed and flailed.

She bit harder.

Ground her jaws together. Like a wild dog savaging a rival.

Harder.

Harder.

She snatched her head away.

He screeched. Blood spurted from the middle of a jagged mess of flesh in his face.

Tess spat. A hunk of nose hit the carpet. She let go of Nat's arms. Let his bucking help her roll away from him.

She clawed at a leg of the table on which Nat waged war between his tiny Confederate and Union armies. With the chair tied to her arms and legs, she couldn't move. Couldn't fight.

She glanced back.

Nat rolled on the floor clutching his face, blood seeping through his fingers. He wailed.

She pulled herself to her feet. She didn't have time to find a knife and try to cut herself free. Not that she'd have been able to reach any of the ties to cut them the way she was bound. She had one option.

As best she could, she leapt into the air, up and backwards. Her chair hit the floor at an awkward angle, but its legs didn't break.

She struggled up again. Glanced over again.

Nat flailed about on the carpet trying to get up.

"Bitch. You fucking bitch!"

Hell, if he got to the table and came at her with a knife now, she was dead.

Again, she jumped backwards.

Again, she crashed to the floor.

Loud cracking sounds bit the air and Tess sprawled amid splintered bits of wooden chair.

She shook her right hand free of the broken chair back. Kicked her feet and shook her left leg loose, but the ties were tight and held her right leg and left arm to the chair's skeleton framework.

She yanked on the wood to try to free herself so she could stand. How could she fight with a three-foot chunk of tree trailing alongside her?

But Nat came at her. Blood streamed down his face, drenching his sweater vest. He looked like a frenzied zombie.

"You fucking bitch! You fucking bitch!" He stormed toward her. Meat cleaver held high to slice into her.

She didn't have her armored gloves. Didn't have her forearm guards. Didn't have a moment to think.

So she didn't.

Like water flowing naturally into a channel, unable to follow any other path, her body reacted.

On her back on the floor, she kicked Nat's legs from under him.

He crashed to the carpet.

But unlike in a third-rate movie, he did not impale himself on his meat cleaver.

On his side, he swung the blade at her.

With a piece of splintered chair leg, she knocked the cleaver from his hand.

She twisted over.

Slammed a kick into his gut.

He clutched his stomach.

Gasped for air.

She rolled towards him.

Smashed the jagged wood down into his bloody face.

On his back, Nat flailed his limbs. They flapped and flapped and flapped.

One by one, his arms and legs dropped.

He gurgled. Spurted blood.

Then lay.

Still.

The broken chair leg stuck up out of his mouth.

Chapter 30

TESS LAY ON the floor for a moment, panting. Her body trembled with nervous energy.

She closed her eyes. Took a long breath in for four seconds, held it for four, then blew it out for four. She repeated the process. She needed to be calm, to have a clear head to formulate an exit strategy.

While she'd been the victim of a crazed killer and had acted in self-defense, she could never admit to what she'd just done. A police investigation might unveil her 'private things.'

Not that doing time was a problem. Unlike Nat, with her skill set, she'd not only survive prison, but thrive there. But how many victims would go unavenged while she was busy being transformed into what the authorities believed was a decent person who made a valuable contribution to society?

She stood and freed herself of the bits of broken chair.

Having grabbed her backpack from the couch, she slipped on a pair of nitrile gloves. She preferred nitrile to latex because of its superior resistance to wear, tears, and chemicals – the ideal prerequisite for clean-up jobs.

Having located the TV remote control, she lowered the volume. The last thing she needed was an irate neighbor banging on the door complaining about the noise. At that moment in the movie, a teenage girl pushed the villain back onto a conveniently placed spike in a wall. Tess snorted. "Yeah, right."

Time for the clean-up.

She walked over to Nat. Stared down at his bloody body. Heaved a weary breath.

That had been too close.

Way too close.

But it wasn't like it could've gone down any other way – she'd done everything she could to identify the killer. When a job took such a sudden, unexpected twist, there was nothing she could do but try to ride it out and pray she struggled through to the other side. Thank God such situations didn't happen often.

Maybe if she hadn't been thrown such a loop by the Bryant Park subway incident, she'd have picked up on something earlier. But there could be no contingency plan for such a fluke encounter and how it had shaken her up. She should just thank her lucky stars she was getting to walk out of here tonight.

Tess snickered.

Luck?

LUCK!

For fuck's sake, what was wrong with her!

'A sudden, unexpected twist'?

Yeah, right. That was what she needed – excuses to make her feel better about herself after screwing up in the most outstandingly dumb way imaginable.

Her gut instinct had warned her something was off. If only she'd listened instead of sentimentalizing this whole ridiculous situation, this predicament would never have arisen.

She glowered at the corpse.

Like her grandpa?

Like her grandpa her ass!

How many times was it going to take before she learned her lesson? Getting close to people got you killed. If nothing else, Shanghai had taught her that. Or so she'd thought.

Yet here she was nearly flat on a slab in the morgue. Again.

And why?

Because some loser reminded her of someone from her past. A past as dead as the person being remembered. Hell, with the tricks the mind played in coloring memories, she wasn't even sure she'd ever lived that life, ever had a grandpa so loving and nurturing.

She heaved a sigh.

When would she learn? It wasn't like it was difficult. In fact, it couldn't be simpler.

No feelings.

Ever.

For anyone.

How many more times would she needlessly have to fight her way out of a deadly situation? This time had

168

been too close. You only got so many chances. Only so many times the cards fell in your favor. The next time she might not be so lucky. And that was why there couldn't be a next time.

No feelings. Ever. For anyone. That had to be her mantra. If she wanted to keep on breathing.

The chair leg made a slurping sound as she pulled it out of Nat's head. While over the body, she took his wallet to let the scene suggest it was a robbery gone sour. An extremely gruesome robbery.

Using Nat's cheese grater, she scraped his face and the piece of bitten-off nose to obliterate the chances of any dental molds being possible.

As the stainless steel teeth chewed up his face, Tess looked into Nat's dead eyes. How wrong had she been. And to what ends people would go to survive.

His facial muscles relaxed, no longer twisted into a raging grimace, he looked like the sweet old man she'd met only a few hours earlier.

Apart from the blood.

Blood she'd spilled.

She gazed at him. She almost felt sorry.

Almost.

With one less monster, the world was a better place. She would close her eyes and sleep well tonight.

She tidied away Nat's arsenal, washed the dishes they'd used for tea and cake, and then collected the broken pieces of chair. She'd dispose of all those later.

In the closet, she found Nat's cleaning supplies. Taking the chlorine bleach over to the body, she doused

169

Nat, head to toe, with pure bleach. That would kill the DNA in any of her hair follicles, saliva, blood, and anything else left behind. She also doused the piece of bloody nose and everywhere else she felt might compromise her situation.

Fingerprints weren't an issue. She'd freely admit to interviewing Nat if need be.

For extra insurance, she pulled a small plastic container from her bag. She glanced around. The couch was as good a place as any – she tossed a broken fingernail onto it that she'd ripped off Marvin Thompson's dead hand two days ago on the Carson kidnapping job. That would give the police something to occupy them and keep them away from her. Especially as they'd never find Thompson's body.

Snagging her wet wipes from her backpack, she popped into the bathroom to clean up so she'd look presentable on the street. Wiping her face in the mirror, she couldn't help but wonder about Nat having a secret. Should she search his apartment for his 'private things'? Why bother? Whatever he'd done in the past, he'd more than paid for it tonight.

Having collected up anything else that might be incriminating, she strolled toward the apartment door, but stopped. She went back to the mantel. Picked up the ticking clock.

She turned it over in her hands. The wood looked like ebony. There was fine engraving on the face. It was probably one of the oldest things Nat owned. Maybe antique. She'd take it. Pawn it. After the expenses of the day, she needed every penny she could lay her hands on to cover all her rents.

She left.

At some point, the neighbors would complain about the smell. The door would be broken down, and Nat's decaying body would be found.

Forensics would process the scene.

Police would interview neighbors.

Suspects and motives would be examined.

Would anyone come knocking at her door?

Chapter 31

EYES CLOSED, TESS bowed her cello, lost in a world of sound and the colors conjured in her mind's eye. Zoltan Kodaly's Solo Cello Sonata Opus 8 enveloped her apartment. The contrasting counterpoints both clashing and delighting in equal measure, the music danced and fought at Tess's command.

A knock at her door almost breached her world but was too far distant to be real.

She played on.

A second knock came louder.

Tess stopped.

Silence.

She strained to hear something. Had she heard a knock? She couldn't have. Had she?

A banging on her door answered her question.

She froze. Why would anyone ever knock on her door? *Who* could ever knock on her door? Other than Bomb, who almost never ventured outside, and the landlord, who was paid direct from her bank so he had no reason to call, no one knew she lived here.

She leaned her cello against her chair and walked through her spartanly furnished living room. Other than the cello and, on a drawer unit near the door, a small glass bowl in which a red Japanese fighting fish swam, there was little to suggest anyone lived here at all.

Keeping it on the security chain, she opened the door two inches and peeked out.

"Oh!" She felt her eyes widen in surprise. And her heart start to pound.

The man said, "I'm sorry. I haven't come at a bad time?"

"No, no. What can I do for you?" If she was going to start getting visitors, she'd have to insist on a peephole in the door in her next place.

He said, "Detective Josh Harding? We met two weeks ago during an investigation into—"

"Yes, I remember. Hello, Detective Harding." She felt her heart slowing, her mind calming. Police officers did not ask if they'd come at a bad time just before reading you your Miranda rights.

He smiled. It was a nice smile. Boyish, yet strong. And those slate-blue eyes drew her even more as the skin crinkled around them.

He said, "Well, since you showed such interest in the case, and actually helped us eliminate certain DNA evidence – you must tell me how you did that, by the way – I thought you might like to know we've apprehended the boyfriend, Ethan Dumfries."

173

"Oh, that's great." She realized she might not appear to be acting quite normally, so she removed the chain and opened the door eighteen inches.

She said, "Sorry, I'm just a little surprised – I didn't know the police were now doing house calls to fill in reporters on case details. Maybe you'd like to finish writing my article while I put my feet up with some Ben and Jerry's and *Murder She Wrote*." She loathed the show, but such a comment bolstered her image of being an unthreatening, gentle woman.

"*Murder She Wrote?* Okay." He laughed. "And here I had you pegged as a *Kill Bill* kinda girl."

She laughed. "All that blood? No, thanks!" She looked at him. He showed no sign of leaving. She was not going to invite him in. Why didn't he get that from the fact she was peeking through a half-closed door? "Was there something else?"

"Well, er… Ha." He shifted his weight awkwardly, like a naughty schoolboy not wanting to confess to what he was up to. "I was kinda hoping you might like to go for a drink some time."

"Oh, er…"

"If I'm stepping on someone else's toes…"

"No, no. Sorry, it's just… talk about a curveball."

He nodded. And waited. "So…?"

"So…" She took a breath. "Sure. That would be nice."

"Fantastic."

"Let me give you my number."

"That's okay." He patted his breast pocket, where many cops kept their notebooks. "Already got it."

"Great. So feel free to give me a call sometime." She smiled and waited for him to leave.

He didn't.

"You know," he said, "if you're not busy now, there's a great little blues bar only two blocks away."

What the hell? Tess stared. "You want to go on a date *now*?"

"Hey, it's just a suggestion. I mean, it's Friday night – you're not out; I'm not out, so…" He shrugged.

"Tell me, Detective Hardy, have you ever dated a woman before?"

His forehead knitted. "Excuse me?"

"A woman. Have you ever dated a woman?"

He smirked. "Yes, I've dated a woman. In fact, more than one. You might say I've dated" – he made air quotes – "women." His cockiness faded. "Though, not at the same time, of course. I'm talking individually. Separately. Er… Monogamously. I don't, er, you know…"

While his bumbling vulnerability was somewhat attractive, she remained silent to let him dig himself a hole and maybe end this here and now.

His face reddening, he said, "Believe it or not, I'm usually quite good at this."

"At screwing up dates?"

He snorted a laugh and then held up his ringless ring finger. "Actually, I, er, guess so."

He locked her with his slate-blue eyes and roguish smile.

That was one hell of a smile.

"Okay," said Tess, "so drawing upon this vast experience of dating women – all separately, with absolutely no crossover – exactly how many seconds did each of those women need to prepare for those dates?"

"Ahhh." He hit himself on the forehead with the palm of his right hand. "Sorry, that's guy mentality for you." He rolled his eyes. "Let me try again – if you aren't busy tonight, would you like a drink at the little blues bar along the street? If so, I can go grab myself a beer and whenever you're ready, you can join me."

This guy just wasn't going to give up.

She said, "I'll tell you what, give me an hour, and have a bottle of cider waiting. Okay?"

He frowned at her. "Cider?"

"It's a drink made from apples."

"Yeah, I know, but—"

"Do you want me to write it down for you?"

"No, it's just, you know, cider...? Who drinks cider?"

She cocked an eyebrow at him. "You're sure you've been quite good at this in the past?"

His face even redder, he flashed a sheepish smile. "Sorry." He tapped his watch, turning to go. "I'll see you in an hour."

She said, "Just one thing."

He turned back, his raised eyebrows asking what she wanted.

"I didn't know I'd given anyone this address." She knew she hadn't. "How did you find me?"

"Hey, I'm a detective. I detected. That's what I do."

She nodded.

"See you in the bar. With a nice cold cider." He waved and blasted that smile at her one last time.

Man, that was a smile.

"Bye." She closed the door. And took the knife from behind her back and replaced it in the small drawer unit upon which Fish sat next to the door.

Tess was always prepared for having to disappear at a moment's notice, so an hour was fifty minutes longer than she needed.

Time to change apartments. And change phone numbers.

The End.

Continue the pulse-pounding Angel of Darkness adventure. Check out what other readers are saying about the next book in the series (book 05).

"A thrilling read from the first to the last page."
Alan Thomas Langridge

"Once again a superb book. I can't wait to get the next one."
Robert Anderson

"This series just keeps getting better. I literally could not put this down. The action seldom slows down enough to catch your breath."
Sheryl Painter

To read *Mourning Scars*, use the link below.

Book 05
http://stevenleebooks.com/wkvr

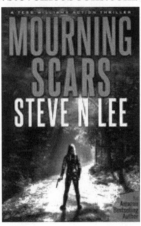

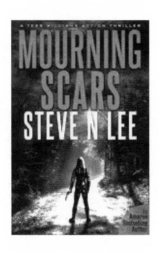

Mourning Scars

Angel of Darkness Book 05

Mourning Scars **extract**

SLOWLY REACHING ACROSS the shelf under his cash register, fingers knotted with arthritis found something cold, hard, unforgiving – his revolver. Chiang had never fired a gun, but no lowlife scum was walking out with his money. Not again. Three robberies in twelve months was just too much.

At his side, Bashe growled. The German shepherd was no fool – he knew there was something wrong too.

Dragging his gaze away from the convex mirror hanging in the far corner of his convenience store, and the shadowy figures reflected in it, Chiang tousled the thick brown fur on Bashe's head.

"Easy, boy."

The big dog shifted restlessly and whined.

Chiang eased his hand back from the shelf. His gun was within reach if he needed it. That was all he needed to know right now.

Standing in front of the register, an old woman with a bulbous nose fussed in her purse. "I'm sorry, Mr. Chiang, I know I've got it somewhere."

She counted out more of her loose change, the skin so thin on her wrinkled hands, the veins stood out like spaghetti under wet tissue paper.

"Is okay, Mrs. Hills. Take your time." Chiang smiled a quavering smile at her and then at her little granddaughter beside her. Sucking on a candy bar she'd only had a few seconds, the little girl already had a ring of chocolate hugging her mouth as if a drunk had applied brown lipstick.

Chiang's gaze returned to the reflection in his security mirror. Three men huddled next to the baking products. Tattooed necks and loping swaggers did not cry 'chef'. What were they doing?

While Mrs. Hills was busy, Chiang surreptitiously slid his hand under the counter to his gun – again – just to check it was within easy reach – again. It was.

Praying he'd never have to use the movement he'd practiced, his gaze shot back to the mirror. He drew his hands down the back of his slacks. When his mouth was so dry, why were his palms so wet?

He stared at the three men. He'd purposefully placed all the baking ingredients at the end of that third aisle, the hardest area in the store to protect, purely because those were the products no one would ever bother stealing. What were those guys doing? What were they waiting for? Did they really believe anyone thought they were discussing which was the best flour to bake cupcakes?

"Well, I'll be darned," said Mrs. Hills. With a laugh, she shook her head. "If I didn't have a twenty-dollar bill in here this afternoon, I'll be a monkey's uncle."

He'd been serving Mrs. Hills for well over ten years. Probably closer to twenty. He'd normally tell her to take what she needed, and give him the money next time, but that wasn't an option today. Today, Chiang needed her to stay as long as possible.

If those guys meant trouble, they'd have caused it already if they didn't care about witnesses. As they were still huddled at the back, they obviously wanted privacy to see through whatever it was they were planning. The longer Mrs. Hills was in the store the better the chances were these guys would get bored and move on.

"Ah!" Mrs. Hills beamed a smile and held twenty dollars aloft. "I knew it was in there somewhere."

His hand trembled as he reached for the money. "I get you anything else, Mrs. Hills?"

"No, that's it, thanks."

Taking his time collecting her change from the register, he glanced up into the mirror. Those men hadn't moved. He needed to buy more time. He held the change out, but didn't drop it into her waiting hand.

He said, "And Mr. Hills? He's good? I don't see him now for nearly two weeks."

She rolled her eyes. "Oh, now there's a tale. Three months he's been waiting to see a consultant about his back. Three months. Well, wouldn't you just know it, no sooner—" She snickered. "Oops, here I am gabbling on and forgetting all about this little one here." She stroked

182

the little girl's head. "Time we should be getting you off to bed, isn't it, sweetheart?"

The girl looked up, but just continued silently sucking her candy bar.

Mrs. Hills looked at Chiang expectantly. He did nothing, so she glanced at his hand holding the money, and then looked back at him, arching her eyebrows.

Chiang dropped the money into her hand. "Thank you, Mrs. Hills."

"We'll catch up tomorrow, when Janie here's back with her mom." She smiled and bundled her granddaughter out of the store.

Chiang watched her every inch of the way.

He wasn't the only one.

The three guys at the back of the store watched too.

Then their gaze swung over to him.

His heart pounding, he hovered his hand over the shelf on which lay his gun. Three robberies in twelve months? There would not be a fourth.

Yes, he could hit the store's panic button and have the police there in minutes, but that wouldn't solve the problem of so many people thinking he was an easy target. As long as they thought that, they'd keep coming back. Well, those people were wrong – he was *not* an easy target.

He kept his hand near his gun. But he had to wait. Had to stay calm. They could be legitimate customers. What would happen to his business if word spread around the neighborhood he'd pulled a gun on three customers just because he didn't like the way three black guys looked?

The three men stalked down the aisle towards the front of the store.

He stared in the mirror. Were they carrying anything? Flour? Sugar? A .45? He couldn't see.

His mouth unbelievably dry, he swallowed hard.

He'd never seen them around here before. So there it was. Proof. Word had spread that he was an easy mark, so now thugs were coming from another neighborhood. Well, were they going to find how wrong they were.

He peered at them over the tops of the shelving units, but could only see their heads.

Hovering over the shelf with his gun, his hand trembled.

The three men sauntered around the corner of the aisle to face him. All tattoos and attitude.

With almost a rehearsed fluidity, each of them reached into their clothing.

Chiang reached onto his shelf.

In a heartbeat, four handguns shot out into the open.

Pushing up on his hind legs, Bashe thumped his huge front paws onto the counter. He fixed his dark eyes on the three men. He snarled.

Chiang aimed at the closet man, a guy with a goatee. "You no take my money again!"

Chiang saw his own gun shaking, so he gripped it in both hands. Still it shook.

"You leave," he continued. "Now! Or I fire. I do. I fire!"

He aimed at the next of the three, a man with a bird of prey tattooed on his chest, visible under his white undershirt. The man planted his foot against the bottom of the door to stop any other customers gaining entry. From outside, no one would see him for a full-length banner advertising an energy drink.

Goatee spoke out of the side of his mouth. "You said he didn't have no piece."

The tattooed guy said, "Yeah, according to Stretch. Don't be laying no blame on me."

Chiang saw them floundering. He shook his gun at them. "No money! I fire!" His thoughts so muddled, he struggled to get English sentences out.

Goatee smiled. He took his aim off Chiang and pointed his pistol at the ceiling. "Hey, we're all cool, man. Ain't no reason for nobody to bleed here tonight, so there ain't."

Goatee waved at his two friends to lower their weapons. They frowned, but they followed his lead and lowered their aims.

The leader smiled at Chiang. "See, everything's cool. Just lay your piece down and everyone will get home safe tonight."

Bashe barked. Chiang dared not even glance at him. But he was thankful he wasn't facing this ordeal alone.

Chiang still trained his trembling gun on them. Before one of them shot him, he could shoot one, maybe even two of them, but no way could he shoot all three. If he wanted to survive this, shooting wasn't an option.

If he played this right, everyone could walk away from this. Everyone. And once word spread about how he'd faced down three goons with guns, people would respect him and leave him alone. Yes, everyone could walk away.

Slowly, he let his gun drop.

The third man smiled. But it wasn't a smile of relief. A sneer of contempt slid across his chubby face.

Chiang whipped his gun back up. Aimed at Chubby Face. Something wasn't right here. He didn't trust these men.

Maybe he was wrong. Maybe fighting was an option. Bashe was so named because of his ravenous appetite – Bashe's mythical namesake was renowned for devouring whole elephants. If Chiang turned Bashe loose, he'd rip one of these men wide open. Could he shoot the other two before they shot him?

What should he do?

His heart hammered.

His breath came in huge gulps.

His gun felt slippery in his sweaty hands.

He couldn't think. Couldn't make sense of the situation. It didn't feel like this was happening. It was as if he were a bystander watching it happen to someone else. And being a bystander, he had no control over it.

What should he do?

"You leave!" He kept his gun up. Shaking. But up.

Goatee kept his smile aimed at Chiang. "Yeah, we'll leave. Just put your piece on the counter so we know no one ain't gonna be shooting no one else in the back."

Chiang's gaze whirled from man to man to man and then back again. What should he do?

He felt a bead of sweat running from his temple down the side of his face.

It was no good. He couldn't fight off all three. Not even with Bashe's help. At least one of them would get a shot off. And if anything happened to Bashe, he'd never forgive himself.

No, if he fired, he'd die. And Bashe too. It was that simple.

So what could he do?

He could press the panic button. Let the police deal with these goons.

But how long would it take for them to arrive?

And that would mean taking a hand off his gun. Fumbling for the button. Waiting and waiting and waiting.

No. He couldn't let the police 'save' him again and have people believe he was weak. He needed to prove he was strong. He needed to prove they had to respect him and never come back. He needed to deal with this alone.

His gaze once more wheeled from face to face to face, looking for a trace of humanity, of honesty, of regret.

Apart from the smiling one with the beard, they looked anxious. Maybe they didn't want to risk shooting any more than he did. Maybe it was all show. Maybe now they respected he was strong too.

So what was he going to do?

Well, their guns were all down. If he put his gun down, there was a good chance they'd leave. Maybe, finally, he'd done enough that word would spread and no one would ever come here looking for easy money ever again.

But could he trust them?

This was a standoff. The four of them couldn't stand like this all night, so mutual trust was the only option.

Chiang looked at the leader again, who smiled and waved for him to lower his gun.

Almost without thinking, Chiang lowered his gun a few inches.

Goatee's smiled broadened. "That's it. No one ain't gonna get shot tonight. But no one."

Bashe snarled.

"Bashe!" Chiang couldn't risk Bashe causing chaos. And he couldn't risk losing him. Not Bashe. Not now. Not when this would be over and everything would be okay in just a few seconds.

Chiang said, "I put down and you leave."

Goatee nodded. "You got it – you put down and we leave."

Chiang put his gun down.

And Goatee whipped his back up and fired.

Chiang slammed back against the cigarette display, a red rose of blood unfurling on his chest, and then crumpled forward.

Bashe leapt onto the counter, teeth bared, ready to rip into soft flesh.

Chubby Face fired.

Bashe yelped and fell to the linoleum in a bloody heap.

"Fucking yapping fucking dog." Chubby Face kissed the chunky gold ring on his trigger finger. "Ain't never let me down yet, have you, baby."

Slumped over the counter, blood oozing out over pale blue laminate, Chiang reached a trembling hand toward his dog. He voice croaked when he spoke. "Bashe."

Bashe struggled to look up at Chiang. The effort forced another yelp.

Goatee nudged Chubby Face. "Get your phone. People gotta see what happens when they fuck with me. But no faces!"

"You think I'm stupid?" With his free hand, Chubby Face snagged his phone from his pocket and filmed the unfolding action.

Goatee stalked toward Chiang, gesturing wildly. "Think you can point a gun at me, motherfucker? Who the fuck d'you think you is dealing with?"

Bashe snarled and tried to stand, tried to defend his master, his friend.

Chubby Face kicked Bashe.

The big dog yelped again.

"Fucking dogs. I hate fucking dogs." Momentarily, Chubby Face trained the camera on his gun and then swung his gun over to aim at Bashe.

Chubby Face said, "Bye bye, doggie."

He fired.

Blood splattered across the linoleum floor and up the side of the counter.

Chubby Face whooped. "Fucking cool, man!"

Chiang shouted, "Bashe!"

Goatee shoved the muzzle of his gun against Chiang's head. "Ain't no slanty-eyed fuck gonna point no piece at me!"

Gasping for breath between words, Chiang's voice rasped. "I ... curse ... you!"

Chiang spat.

Goatee's gun boomed.

Chapter 2

Shadows lurking in the darkness all about her, Tess Williams clomped along the asphalt path which led to the Lake and Bethesda Fountain, her usual athletic grace purposefully replaced by the clumsy meandering of someone seemingly worse for drink. As she neared them, some shadows formed recognizable shapes – trees, bushes, fountains, benches – while others were still so mired in gloom they remained forever shrouded in mystery.

She glanced at the flower beds on either side of the path – just a mass of dark blobs. And they looked so lovely by day.

The wind whistled through the trees and swirled some of the fallen brown leaves about her feet.

She clomped on. She'd chosen these shoes especially because of how loud they made her footfalls on hard surfaces, but alone in the dead of night, she was amazed at just how noisy they were.

Patches of dark cloud hanging motionless in the sky, Tess struggled to see the moon or any stars.

While the park was a glorious place to visit during daylight hours, it was a nightmare place to be at night. Why would any of those women have been here alone after sunset? Stupidity. Ignorance. Intoxication. Whatever the reason, you could almost say they'd got what they deserved. Almost.

A chill wind forced a shudder from her. Instead of zipping up her black leather jacket, as she would've liked, she unzipped it fully. She looked down at her cleavage bursting out of her little white top. Surely that was enticing enough.

She dawdled, dragging her feet so they scraped on the path to make even more noise and alert anyone in the vicinity to her presence. She threw in a little stumble and then giggled at having tripped – let anyone spying from the shadows think she was drunk and even more vulnerable than she'd at first appeared.

The wind rustled the leaves in the heavy trees lining the path.

Tess shivered. She didn't know if it was the cold or anxiousness. Probably a little of both.

At night, the park offered way too many places from behind which someone could attack the unwary. And they had. The proof was all over the media. But not just attacked them. No, this guy was twisted. Even by New York City standards. His story certainly wouldn't feature in one of those cozy police procedural shows the TV corporations loved to set in the city. No way. He was way too sick for primetime.

A big dark blob loomed on her left. Seven feet tall and pear shaped. Probably a bush. Probably. But even if it was, who lurked behind it: a mugger, a rapist, a psycho with a meat cleaver…?

The wind howled through the darkness.

And the shadowy blob moved.

Tess gasped, her heart pounding in her chest as if it were trying to break through her ribcage and run for safety.

Even though she was expecting to be attacked, wanting to be attacked, it didn't stop icy dread crawling up her spine.

She squinted, trying to see more clearly, trying to put form to that which was shrouded in blackness.

Was it a bush?

Really?

Or was it…?

***

To continue reading *Mourning Scars* (book 05), use the link below.

Book 05

http://stevenleebooks.com/wkvr

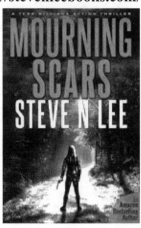

Free Library of Books

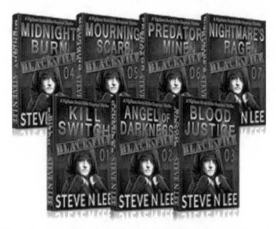

Thank you for reading *Midnight Burn*. To show my appreciation of my readers, I wrote a second series of books exclusively for them – each Angel of Darkness book has its own *Black File*, so there's a free library for you to collect and enjoy.

A FREE Library Waiting for You!

Exclusive? You bet! You can't get the *Black Files* anywhere except through the links in the *Angel of Darkness* books.

Start Your FREE Library with *Black File 04*.
http://stevenleebooks.com/vy0d

Make Your Opinion Count

Dear Thriller Lover,

Do you have a few seconds to spare?

It is unbelievably difficult for an emerging writer to reach a wider audience, not least because less than 1% of readers leave reviews. Hard to believe, isn't it? Of one hundred readers, maybe - that's 'maybe' - one reader will post a few words.

Please, will you help me by sharing how much you enjoyed this book in a short review?

It only takes a few seconds because it only needs a handful of words. I'll be ever so grateful.

Don't follow the 99% – stand out from the crowd with just a few clicks!

Thank you,

Steve

Copy the link to post your review

http://stevenleebooks.com/zlj1

Free Goodies – VIP Area

See More, Do More, Get More!

Do you want to get more than the average reader gets? Every month I send my VIP readers some combination of:

- news about my books

- giveaways from me or my writer friends

- opportunities to help choose book titles and covers

- anecdotes about the writing life, or just life itself

- special deals and freebies

- sneak behind-the-scenes peeks at what's in the works.

Get Exclusive VIP Access with this Link.

http://stevenleebooks.com/wcfl

Angel of Darkness Series

Book 01 – Kill Switch

This Amazon #1 Best Seller explodes with heart-stopping thrills, as Tess Williams rampages across Eastern Europe in pursuit of a gang of sadistic kidnappers.

http://stevenleebooks.com/ein6

Book 02 – Angel of Darkness

In Manhattan, Tess hunts a crazed sniper in a story bursting with high-octane action and nail-biting suspense.

http://stevenleebooks.com/tz0q

Book 03 – Blood Justice

Intrigue, betrayal and red-hot action surround a senseless murder. Thrust into the deadly world of crime lords and guns-for-hire, only justice-hungry Tess can unveil the killer in this gripping action-fest.

http://stevenleebooks.com/jpwb

Book 04 – Midnight Burn

Even 'unstoppable' killing machines have weaknesses. Discover Tess's as she hunts a young woman's fiendish killer in this action-packed tale of murder, mayhem and mystery.

http://stevenleebooks.com/mboq

Book 05 – Mourning Scars

Crammed with edge-of-your-seat action, this adventure slams Tess into the heart of a gang shooting and reveals the nightmare that drove her to become a justice-hungry killer.

http://stevenleebooks.com/wkvr

Book 06 – Predator Mine

Bursting with blazing-hot action, this page-turner plunges Tess into the darkest of crimes. And dark crimes deserve even darker justice. Discover just how dark a hero can be when Tess hunts a child killer.

http://stevenleebooks.com/8u5n

Book 07 – Nightmare's Rage

If someone killed somebody you loved, how far would you go to get justice? Vengeance-driven Tess is about to find out in an electrifying action extravaganza.

http://stevenleebooks.com/4f98

Book 08 – Shanghai Fury

Tess Williams is a killer. Cold. Brutal. Unstoppable. Discover how her story begins, how a fragile woman becomes a dark hero, how an innocent victim becomes a merciless killing-machine.

http://stevenleebooks.com/gr19

Book 09 – Black Dawn

Everything ends. Tess has sacrificed her life to protect the innocent by hunting those that prey upon them. Now, that life is over so she can build a life for herself. Or can she...?

http://stevenleebooks.com/blq7

Book 10 – Die Forever

While hunting a brutal gang, Tess is thrust into one of the deadliest places on the planet for one of her deadliest battles. With the clock ticking, how can she get out alive?

http://stevenleebooks.com/5h6y

About Steve N. Lee

Steve lives in Yorkshire, in the north of England, with his partner Ania and two cats who adopted them.

Picture rugged, untamed moorland with Cathy running into Heathcliff's arms – that's Yorkshire! Well, without the running. (Picture jet-black bundles of fur – that's their cats.)

He's studied a number of martial arts, is a certified SCUBA diver, and speaks 10 languages enough to get by. And he loves bacon sandwiches smothered in brown sauce.

Use the link below to learn more – some of it true, some of it almost true, and some of it, well, who really knows? Why not decide for yourself?

http://stevenleebooks.com/a5w5

Made in the USA
Columbia, SC
07 August 2022

64822402R00121